The Day the Mirror Cried

Eileen –

Enjoy my

book – loved

meeting you –

Saundra

Saundra G Kelley
Jonesborough Storyteller

Published by:
Southern Yellow Pine (SYP) Publishing
4351 Natural Bridge Rd.
Tallahassee, FL 32305

www.syppublishing.com

This is a work of fiction. Names, characters, places, and events that occur either are the products of the author's imagination or are used fictitiously. Any resemblance to actual persons, places, or events is purely coincidental.

The contents and opinions expressed in this book do not necessarily reflect the views and opinions of Southern Yellow Pine Publishing, nor does the mention of brands or trade names constitute endorsement.

ISBN-10: 1940869234

ISBN-13: 978-1-940869-23-0

Front Cover Design: Jim Hamer

Printed in the United States of America
First Edition
August 2014

Dedication

This book is dedicated to my fellow storytellers in the
Jonesborough Storytellers Guild, and to beautiful
Jonesborough, Tennessee,
Storytelling Capital of the World.

Contents

Dedication iii

Acknowledgments.. vii

Preface... ix

Part I - REFLECTIONS IN STORY... 1

   Held In Thrall... 3

   The Day the Mirror Cried 5

   Channels of Ecstasy 16

   Only in my Dreams 17

   Slice of Life.. 22

   The Ship's Lantern 23

   Night Call 29

   The Curse of Stinkbug Hollow 30

   Tempest... 36

   Ice Palace at the Top of the World.. 37

   Ultimate Orgasm 44

   Laugh at the Moon No More... 45

   Wrecking Ball 56

   Intruder... 57

   Cloud Dancing 59

   Ms. Ruby's Red Carpet 60

   Ignition... 67

   Emerald Forest 68

   Iris Bound... 72

Part II - SOUTHERN TOWNS AND ODD MEMORIES 73

   The Legend of Tate's Hell, 1875 75

   Crone Am I 79

   Smooth Operator 80

   On the Track.. 105

   Suspicious Remains 106

   The Last Cypress Tree 116

   Blue Lightning 117

   Moment In Time 121

   Gator Giggin' in Blackwater Swamp....................................... 122

   Raptor's Lament.. 127

PART III - RUMINATION 129
  Lessons for the Errant 131
  Almost Left Behind 132
  Butterfly in a Box 135
  Third Grade Drama Queen 136
  Discord 141
  The Glass Case 142
  Dandelion's Gold 145
  Due Diligence 146
  Suspension 149
  Toni Boyd Wise Woman 150
  Late Winter Snow 152
  Secret Places 153
  Reflections Over Water 155
  Life of a River 156
  Lost Mountain 159
  Fair Weather, My Friend 160
  Heat 162
  An Affair of the Heart 163
  Fallen Stones 166
  Snow on the Mountain 167
  Sister, Let me Share your Trouble 169
  Broken 170
  Break of Day 173

Acknowledgments

A collection such as this could not come about without the support of some very special people. As always, my daughters, Kitty Kelley Draa and Kristy Noel Kelley, were my champions, urging me to move forward with my work.

Most of the stories in this collection found their beginnings as spoken word, growing as I told them, and have not been set to the written page until now. Converting them from the oral tradition to the written was a challenge, but SYPP publisher, Terri Gerrell, and her staff were by my side all the way through, unrepentant in determination, unflagging in support.

I am indebted to Ben Dugger, award-winning Tennessee poet, for reviewing these poems and encouraging me to cut them to the merest bone of meaning with the most beautiful of words. A big thank you to Andrea Brunais and Rose Klix for reading the short stories and offering significant suggestions to make them read better.

Thank you to Dot Jackson, author of *Refuge, an Appalachian novel*, who allowed me to base The Ship's Lantern on a dream. Thanks also to Pam Miller, PhD and fellow storyteller, who really does favor Susan Sarandon and has the most lovely manners in all the world. My apologies for making her character implode in The Legend of Stinkbug Hollow.

Preface

As an author and an oral tradition storyteller, stories are my stock in trade. It wasn't until I began writing my own stories for telling, however, that I began to feel a different relationship to them. When one draws a story thought from the air, lays it on an arc, defines its beginning, middle, and end, and then begins to express it orally, there is a completely different dynamic than when one writes it all down, prints it off, ponders, corrects, ponders some more, and sends it to the publisher.

A case in point is <u>*Ice Palace at the Top of the World*</u>. That story dropped into my fertile psyche on a windy, snowy day. I was literally trapped inside but able to watch the snow drift and then pour from the sky. Birds played in it the whole day, taking great joy in whatever it was they found there. One downy woodpecker settled into the crook of my silver maple and rested there for a long time, on occasion taking a sip from the snow banked around his little body. Mourning doves covered the ground, as cardinals, blue jays, Carolina wrens, titmouse, and chickadees entertained me from sun up to sundown. During that time, I began to feel stranded on my little ridge, and it became my ice palace at the top of the world. The story grew from there with nothing more than rungs in my mind, until finally, I cast its bones on the arc. The next chance I had to tell stories, I trotted that one out purely as an oral tale. Now, I have it written in literary format, frozen into a moment in time in this book, but for a while, it was fluid and great fun to work with.

I tell you this because these stories and the poetry that I have included are here to provoke one to thought.

Enjoy and think about these slightly weird stories, the people and thoughts that fill them, and find your own place within.

Part I

REFLECTIONS IN STORY

Held In Thrall

An ephemeral blur
of exquisite pale-green settled
on my window screen.

Luna, Luna Moth!

Seen from the inside,
an undercarriage of delicate tracery,
intricate webbing,
infinitesimally small feet
clinging tightly—

Ah, not one, but two—
a mating pair engaged
in that most primeval of rituals,
rendered
as fragile and lovely
as their conjoined bodies.

Revealing no movement
or sexual pleasure
to my prurient eye,
they held one another
for a night and a day.

I watched—
a captivated
voyeur….

Intimate observation laid bare
something coy, yet free—
rapt by an essential knowing
beyond ecstasy.

Luna, Luna Moth!

With the rising sun
Luna's mate was gone.

Still, she clung to the screen
with an aching stillness;
then she too drifted away
to bear new life
and then to die.

Luna, Luna Moth!

The Day the Mirror Cried

I grew up in the 1950s in a small, university town in the Deep South. On those rare occasions when the unexpected erupted in our community, it sometimes forced us to confront vile reality; we wondered how on earth it could happen in our perfect little town.

The university sustained and contributed to our town's self-concept; the culture it represented was almost untouchable, as were the people it venerated. Ideas were tolerated as long as they were generated by stodgy, respected professors, resulting in published, classroom tomes.

The main entrance, with its black wrought-iron gates, guarded the mysterious temple of learning. The children of the town's most respected families passed through those gates, to emerge as polished model citizens, equipped to maintain their proper places in society.

University presidents and professors frequently married into local society, and then built elegant homes next to mansions of pre-Civil War era vintage in which to raise their broods, thereby perpetuating a highly venerated way of life.

Most town folk revered the gracious mansions and cherished the fine old families who lived there, and what they represented. When one of the great houses crumbled through neglect or under the bulldozer's shovel, the elders in our community paused to remember, telling stories about the families that once lived there. Rumored to be haunted, some of those old homes contained mysteries still unsolved and nearly forgotten. They spoke of troubled histories, expressed in hushed, reverential tones of respect for those long gone—even though some still lived. My memories of one of those old houses are vivid and personal. My mother, a home-school teacher with the university laboratory school, taught a young girl named Amy who had severe

5

asthma and allergies. Frequently housebound, she missed school most often during hurricane season when it seemed to rain all the time. We called the time of storms and torrential rains monsoon season and often wondered if our town and all of the people in it might float away some day. Folks like Amy suffered torture as mold shrouded every surface in that hot, humid climate with the gray-green fuzz to which she was allergic.

The shabby Victorian mansion where Amy lived was the lone survivor of the great houses that once lined Winthrop Avenue. Though surrounded by plain, one-story, concrete block student apartments, the large, imposing two-story house defied change and continued to dominate the neighborhood. It was famous for the stained glass window on the second floor landing, said to be priceless. Situated only a block from the entrance to the university, people often drove by in the late evening on the way to the symphony; others, coming on it unexpectedly, slowed down to see the softly glowing window with its osprey shrouded by heavy gray moss; some stopped in the middle of the road to stare at it in awe.

The overgrown yard was a dark, secluded jungle, and through it ran an inlaid, stone walkway leading up to the worn, red brick steps. These steps were wide and flanked by low concrete enclosures on which sat huge, snarling lions ripped from stone. Old live oaks and sabal palms intruded onto the dark porch, and pots of withered ferns crowded together on a peeling, ornate, cast iron table under deep windows covered in dusty, ivory lace.

Each time we visited the house, I expected a crotchety butler to open the imposing front door, not the tiny, bird-like sisters with the soft, genteel Southern voices who let us in. Twins in their late sixties named Martha and Mable, the sisters were the daughters of a former president of the university who was also a popular Presbyterian lay speaker. Neither had ever married, and both had lived in the old house all of their lives. I never could tell them apart, so I called them both "ma'am," just to be on the safe side.

They really were identical—mousy gray hair cut in bobs to just below their ears; short bangs framed soft, wrinkled, round faces that always seemed to be freshly powdered, and 24K gold, clip-on earrings pinched their drooping earlobes. Year-round they both wore gold wire-rimmed glasses perched on their noses and a never-ending array of faded, cotton housedresses, worn with sensible, oxford-style shoes and opaque stockings.

The sisters were always courteous when we came, but it was obvious to both my mother and me that they resented having anyone from the outside in their house, even though it was obvious they loved their niece Amy, and wished her well. Conversation with them never got beyond the polite talk expected when paying a courtesy call. It's a wonder Mother didn't drop her card on the tarnished tray in the foyer, but she never did—she understood them somewhat—since she also, was a combination of the town-and-gown society. She respected their desire for privacy, but when it came to Amy, she was all business. The child had to have a proper education, and she was there to make sure she got it, unless Amy was too sick to cooperate, which sometimes happened during hurricane season.

Inside, the house was cavernous with high ceilings and trim of rich, dark wood. Some said it was sweet gum cut from the property during construction. The rooms were musty and mysterious, lit by dull, bare lightbulbs suspended from cracked, ornate ceilings. The dim light softened the fussy, faded elegance of the antique furnishings, creating an illusion of grandeur in rooms that spoke of a real past and an uncertain future. The smell of old books, old clothes, mildew, and lavender pervaded every room; my mother often expressed her concern at Amy having to live with the pervasive odors. Surely, it would be better for her in a nice, clean, modern school building with a school nurse nearby, than in this musty old house, but her comments went unheeded.

When Mother first began teaching Amy she took me along for the purpose of socialization for the child. The old, decaying house quickly became one of my favorite places to visit. I vastly preferred it to the '50s style bungalows and sleek ranch houses with no history and no ghosts. My mother said I loved it because it provided plenty of fodder for my overactive imagination. Had she known what was going to happen there, she might never have let me go at all….

An ornate gilded mirror seat dominated the foyer just to the right of the front door. It was almost as tall as the 12-foot high ceiling, its silver face tarnished and streaked. I was fascinated by it, and I stood in front of it each time I visited, mesmerized by the wavy images. I thought I could see movement in its depths, especially on rainy days, and I spent hours fantasizing about it.

Amy's room was upstairs. At the top of the stairs on the landing, overlooking the tree-lined avenue below, and just barely visible from the outside during the day, was the famous, stained glass window. It was the family masterpiece, said to be a gift from the university when the old president finally retired. Designed by a professor from the art department, it portrayed a large osprey framed by a sabal palm tree. Held in the raptor's talons was a tiny marsh mouse, eyes wide with fear. When the sun was out during the day, the hallway turned a strange shade of watery green and it looked as though the great bird might come to life, eat the mouse, and crash right through that window. The diffusion of greenish light from the window, mixed with the odd smells and threadbare carpet, made it a scary place to be. For some strange reason, I rather liked that bird, but while the window pulled me in, I seldom lingered on the landing, nurturing strange notions about it. Once, in a nightmare, I dreamed the osprey flew down the hallway, chasing its prey, and that I was the mouse he was chasing.

One of the doors was padlocked. On those rare occasions when she was willing to answer my questions, Amy told me that it was Edmund's room, but nothing more. Later, I learned that Edmund Peavey, PhD, had been a friend of the family and a professor at the university. No one had seen him in years, but rumors about him surfaced on occasion. Just after she began tutoring Amy, I overheard my mother and grandmother talking about him in a whispered conversation. That little chat ceased abruptly when I sneezed and betrayed my presence, but I never forgot his name or the sense of mystery that surrounded it.

I had heard enough to know that the handsome and courtly Professor Peavey came to stay at the house not long after the twins' father died. He boarded there as a single gentleman, and as there were no other boarders, this created a situation which provoked gossip amongst the church ladies at the First Presbyterian Church, but it was never mentioned in either of the sisters' presence. People saw them frequently at the theater and the symphony with the courtly professor, and life seemed gay, indeed. I could just imagine how they must have looked then: prim, their hair done up in old-fashioned styles, with sensible shoes and sensible, small pieces of very nice jewelry—not too much—just right.

At some point, things changed for the sisters when the professor left town suddenly, and they withdrew abruptly from society. Nobody knew what happened to him—he simply stopped teaching one semester. According to the part of the conversation I overheard, apparently he just picked up and left, ostensibly to return to his home up north.

As for Amy, rumor had it that Amy mysteriously *arrived* at the house fourteen years earlier, around the same time the professor left. The maiden aunts, neither of whom had ever been around small children, had to deal with the care of an infant, almost as if by magic. I could just imagine baby Amy arriving in the middle of the night and the befuddled aunts trying to care for her.

As word spread that a baby was in the household, the whole town went into an uproar. The ladies' missionary society arrived with bottles, diapers, homemade baby food, advice, and questions. Graciously received and properly thanked, they were packed off, their questions unanswered. Many were miffed—they had been guests in that home for years, and now, to be turned away? It was unthinkable!

The town saw petitions filed, and meetings held at *both* the Episcopal and Presbyterian churches downtown and interventions begun, but baby Amy stayed on with the sisters, who grew more reserved by the year. Any hint of scandal and the sisters withdrew even more. The gossipmongers never found the answers to the many questions they asked, and the sisters got their wish—solitude. Amy, however, was always a topic of interest.

My mother was Amy's home-school teacher and was frequently bombarded with questions about the girl, but Mother refused to answer them. The townspeople wanted to know who Amy's mother was, suspecting she was perhaps the daughter of their long-lost sister, Maria, the one who ran away before she graduated from high school. Folks wondered too, why, with the advances of modern medicine in the field of asthma treatment, didn't the child's health improve? And what, they asked on rare occasions, ever happened to the good professor?

By the time I met Amy, she was quiet but growing rebellious. When my mother and I were there, she asked countless questions about the movies and the stars she worshiped in seclusion. We took magazines to her and tried to answer her questions as best we could, but we could only provide a taste of the world we knew. I could tell my mother was worried.

As I grew older, visiting Amy became a chore. Entering my teens, I, too, grew rebellious and learned to hate the dark old house and the gaudy oleanders that grew rampant around it, and I hated the scent of lavender in any form. In addition, I was tired of trying to set a good example for Amy. It was obvious she wanted nothing more from me than gossip and my magazines. On the days we were to visit, she watched for us from the window seat in her room, a shadow barely visible behind the crusty, ivory lace curtains. Her pale skin, huge dark eyes, and dark red lips—we never knew where she got that red lipstick or why her aunts tolerated it—haunted everyone who saw her looking out of her window. The townspeople grew to think of her as that "poor girl on Winthrop Avenue."

The odd smell in the house faded somewhat over time, except on the days when it rained. My mother and I always bathed and washed our clothing after visits to the mansion, but I declared the odor stayed in my nostrils from visit to visit. Somehow, the smells went beyond the tattered furniture, moldy rugs, decaying wood, old people, and older clothes.

One rainy day near the semester's end, my mother was ill with a headache. To help her, I took the lesson plans to Amy's house, catching the bus for the short ride. Dampness permeated every surface on the bus—the plastic seats were damp and beads of water covered the slick blue metal surrounding the windows. I drew finger pictures on the glass and watched them disappear in streams of water rolling down the window.

As we neared the house, I pulled the call-string to signal I wanted to get out. When the big blue bus skidded to a stop, rainwater swirled around its wheels in eddies, nearly sweeping me off my feet as I missed the step in my haste. I got my footing and ran up the walkway to the relative safety of the house, my heart pounding in my throat at the near miss.

I ran past the gaudy, pink, white, and red oleanders, their blossoms drooping in the rain, up the steps past the angry-looking lions with their peeling paint, and knocked on the door. The lightbulb above my head danced and swayed from side to side, occasionally banging into the

10

porch siding, and I feared it would shatter before I got into the house. A chill wind whipped around my legs, and my hair clung in damp strings around my face as I waited.

At long last one of the ladies opened the door. The odor assailed me as soon as I stepped into the hall, moldy humidity flooding through the opening to join the wind gusts outside.

She calmly asked me to wait in the foyer and then went slowly up the stairs to get Amy. I watched her go, just glad to be out of the howling storm that had picked up again on my arrival at the house. I turned away and waited next to the tall mirror, water forming a puddle on the floor at my feet.

Rain came down in gray sheets outside as the storm gathered momentum, and thunder shook the house enough to make the lightbulb high above me jiggle in its socket. Lightning struck nearby and hearing a sound behind me, I turned to face the mirror. Its surface, always tarnished and streaked from years of neglect, cracked before my eyes. Staring in horror, I watched as water dribbled down its surface and pooled in the dust on the seat at the bottom.

As the mirror cried, I saw figures moving inside. Mesmerized, I stood there, glued to the drama playing out before my eyes. I could see a lovely young woman with dark hair like Amy's in bed with a baby, and Amy's aunts standing outside the door, talking. I could see what must have been Edmund's head peeking out of the door by the big stained glass window, and instinctively, I knew he was listening.

Suddenly Amy appeared behind me, startling me, and I gasped in relief. "Look," I said, "the mirror cracked when that bolt of lightning struck. It's crying!"

Then I looked at the mirror again and saw the figures still moving and pointed to its surface saying, "Amy, see, it's cracked, and can you see the people in there?"

Amy looked at the cracked mirror and shrugged. She took the papers from me and started walking toward the stairs, saying nothing. Suddenly, she swung around and said, "It always cries when the rains come in summer. Aunt Martha says that's when my mother died. I think the mirror cries for her." She left me standing there, mouth wide open in shock, and went up the stairs without saying another word.

I could hardly wait to reach home to tell my mother what I had seen. I didn't even think about the rushing water sucking me down into the belly of the earth and ran right over it. By the time I got to the bus stop, I was drenched again but thought nothing of it. On the way home, I kept my arms crossed against my chest and held my legs close together. I thought I might explode from the tension of it all. The short ride took forever.

Damp and agitated, I ran into my parent's darkened bedroom. Soaked to the skin and babbling in my excitement, I flopped down on the bed beside my mother, startling her from a deep sleep. I slowed down when I remembered she was ill, but nothing could keep me from sharing my news.

Groggy with sleep, my poor mother sat up and stared at me. Then, before I could say another word, she made me change clothes and towel my hair dry. Only then did she allow me to come back for what I hoped would be a mother-daughter talk.

Snuggled up on the bed beside her, I told my mother what I had seen in the mirror and what Amy had told me. She listened patiently, showing little emotion until I was finished. Then she carefully put her head back down on the pillow and absent-mindedly sent me to my room to do my homework; she never said a word that day about Amy, the sisters, or the house on Winthrop Avenue. Somehow, I missed the odd way she stared at me as I shared my news.

When I left the room, it was with a sense of letdown. Maybe what I saw was just an illusion, but I couldn't get it out of my mind, and I didn't think what Amy told me was a lie at all.

I could hardly wait to get to school the next day and was just about to run out the door when my mother stopped me.

"Roseanne, don't tell anyone what you saw and heard at Amy's yesterday. Promise me," she said. She held me there with her eyes until I made the promise I couldn't break, and then she let me go.

I found it difficult to sit still in class that day and was eager to run home so I could go to the big house with my mother. However, she had other plans and told me to stay home and do my homework.

Seeing the look on my face, she smiled and said, "Just do as I say, Roseanne. I'll be home in just a little while, and then we'll talk. I promise. Call your father at the store if you need anything." With that, she straightened her hat, picked up her purse, and left the house, a determined tilt to her head, her heels clicking on the sidewalk.

Although I was pleased my mother felt well enough to attend to her students again, I was not happy to see her gather the books and papers up and leave without me. When my mother walked like that, she looked like an admiral on a ship going to war, and I knew that I, her first lieutenant and chief informant, was going to miss the action. I dawdled with my homework, sitting on pins and needles all afternoon waiting for her; when she came home, I was in for a surprise.

When she returned, she said, "Amy is going to a private school in Atlanta, Roseanne. I talked with Martha and Mable about it; Dr. Segree agrees with us, and we all feel it's the best thing for her. They have relatives there who can check on her, and perhaps a change of scenery would be helpful. She is excited about it and will leave soon. It's all planned."

That's the sum-total of the information I received, and I felt betrayed. My mother had just pulled off something big without me. After several years of faithfully visiting Amy—all the questions, and what I was sure was my big clue, I felt I deserved more. She wouldn't tell me anything else, no matter how much I pleaded with her. What was up? What about her promise to "tell all?"

We visited Amy one last time before she left for her new school. The sun was out and the oleanders were a riot of color surrounding the drab old mansion.

For the first time since we met, Mother and I took Amy out for lunch and then downtown to P.W. Wilson's to buy some clothes on her aunt's revolving charge account. I was so full of questions I thought I would blow up from the pressure, but Amy was distant, and my mother was unusually subdued as well. Later, I wondered if Amy knew that what she told me had started all of this. Even I didn't know for certain, but I had my suspicions; after all, I was the one who saw the mirror cry.

Two weeks after she left, the strange truth finally came out, and the stink of it filled every room in our town. With Amy safely away in school, the police finally visited the house, thanks to my mother. They requested entry to look for an escaped felon. Wary, the sisters could hardly refuse a warrant, and the search was on. What they found—it was raining that day, too, cats and dogs—was two bodies behind the locked door in the room beside the stained glass window: Professor Edmund Peavey, PhD, and a young woman who turned out to be their

13

younger sister, Maria, lying mummified in lavender, side by side in the bed where Amy was born.

The woman was Amy's mother, lying in death by Amy's father, Edmund. It's a wonder the malodorous smells didn't knock the police right off their feet, but they were tough men in those days and went right in.

I later found out the lovely Maria died shortly after Amy was born and never left her bedroom again. Upon questioning the aunts, the police discovered that Maria, heavily pregnant, had shown up on their then elegant doorstep on an angry, blustery night some fourteen years earlier. The sisters, horrified by the unexpected arrival of their errant sister, but wanting to avoid scandal, took her in and secluded her in her old room on the second floor. After Amy's birth and Maria's death, they took the baby, covered Maria's body in canvas with dried lavender to mask the odor, padlocked the room, and left their sister there.

They told the police that Edmund, who was indeed Amy's father, died some time later. They laid him in the bed with Maria, and he decomposed beside her, a fitting journey in the aunts' minds because he had been lover to them all.

The unfortunate Maria met the handsome and cultured Edmund at a party in Savannah, Georgia, where she was working as a bartender. After a brief affair and learning of the more prosperous sisters in Louisiana, the courtly professor left her behind without a penny, headed south, and never looked back.

The elegant Edmund wooed first one, then the other of the aunts, and never told them of the sister he had impregnated prior to coming to them. It took very little persuasion for the ladies to allow the handsome professor to join them as a renter and for some time, life was gay, if not rather daring, indeed. That is, until the night Maria arrived in the storm.

That night, when the door opened, Maria collapsed in labor on the oriental carpet in the foyer at the base of the tall mirror seat. Fearful that someone might have seen her, they quickly closed the big door and got the good Edmund to help them move their sister up the stairs; together, they delivered the child, and in a lucid moment, Maria named the baby Amy.

Before she died early the next morning, Maria asked for Edmund. When he refused to come, she told her sisters who he was. One can only imagine the sense of betrayal they must have experienced. They shared everything they had with the man, and in the end, he deceived them all. It was then they began to look for a way to assist him to an early demise. Avid murder mystery readers in their youth, the gentle ladies eventually found the way growing in their own yard. They began slipping gradually increasing amounts of poisonous, dried oleander leaves into his food until his heart simply stopped beating.

Such a relief it was to the two of them to finally dispatch him to their sister's resting place. Surely, the two miscreants deserved one another.

The mirror told the tale, however, because each time it rained the story played again and again, crying through the pain of it, hoping to find someone to listen and right an old wrong. I was the person who saw the figures moving in the mirror's face, and together, my mother and I finally solved the mystery of the big house on Winthrop Avenue, the day the mirror cried.

Channels of Ecstasy

Sounds
infuse body, mind, and soul—
an undulating world of
rhythmic mystique
and ancient wisdom.

Singing, speaking, crying, screaming, emoting
come from spirit—a pulsating xylophone
of beat and tonal inflection.

Sometimes clear—more often implied,
sounds traverse unseen airwaves
into swirling canals mysterious,
passing through our known universe
to worlds unseen.

Only in my Dreams

Going to my favorite spot of an evening to watch the sun go down—a brackish inlet near the Gulf of Mexico—I settled in for the nightly ritual. The sun slid slowly down over still, gray waters, lulling me as always, until I saw a ripple in the water. Alligator? That would come as no surprise—they peopled the swampy area just as I did, but no, the head was rounded. An otter probably. No, not an otter, something bigger, but what?

Shallow ripples spread around the being that swam my direction at a leisurely pace. It seemed as though I might be under observation. A shiver snaked down my back, but I stayed where I was, mesmerized as the mysterious entity glided toward me. Attuned to the mysteries of the wild, I was eager to see what earth mother offered me that day, but as the creature came toward me, something akin to fear roiled in my belly. *What's this,* I said to myself, *you, the adventurer afraid of a small critter in a pond?*

When it got to the shallows, I could see this was a seal, a big one. Certainly not a native, it was like nothing I had seen in these waters. A graceful swimmer, its flippers were awkward when they slapped the mud on land.

I scooted back onto the hood of my car and then back toward the windshield. There was no time to get in, nor did I want to.

Making its way to where I sat above dense, marsh grass, the big animal slid upright and stared at me, whiskers quivering, huge dark eyes speaking volumes that I couldn't understand. It balanced on the thick, flapped tail and muscular, front flippers, watching me with an unwavering stare.

Seeming to come to a decision, the creature slid down into the grass and rolled over with the innate grace of a dancer. When the seal

17

came back around, the fine fur came loose like an opera cape and fell to the ground. In its midst stood a man, strong boned, perhaps six feet tall with jet black hair and dark brown eyes. Every part of him was anatomically correct, make no mistake; unbidden, my breath came in gasps. A shape-shifter here, on Turkey Point?

He moved toward me, not as a seal, but as a most desirable man. That he was aroused was obvious, and from the dampness I felt between my legs, so was I. I felt no fear—this meeting felt pre-destined, and I welcomed the mystery of it.

Quickly, my mind reviewed what I knew about shape shifters from the sea: supposedly, they are fairytale creatures, fabrications of imagination from the days of Celtic heroes and strange water creatures, not in this day of cars and computers. Those were my thoughts, but the hand that touched mine was not a fabrication. It was warm, vital, demanding. I let him lift me from the car and down to the grass, then hand in hand, we made our way to a secluded cove under the longleaf pines. I asked no questions and hesitated only a moment. What if…?

Soft winds caressed bare skin as we made love into the night. Often I dreamt about lovemaking of this kind, but never knew it for myself. At last, we slept, wrapped in one another's arms till the sun rose. When he pulled away from me and made to leave, I cried out, "Don't go."

"I must go."

"I will take your skin," I said. I felt the warm sealskin at my back. "Then you'll never be able to leave."

"Give it to me, my love, and I will come again when the moon is full." Through tears of frustration and spent passion, I moved and let him take the skin. Watching him slide into it with little effort, I knew he had done this many times before. "Before you leave, tell me how you came to be here."

He turned then, a seal again, and spoke to my heart, "I live in your dreams, my love, in your dreams."

My body sated, it was as though a part of me glided gently out of sight when he swam away. I fell into a deeply satisfying sleep, nurtured by birdcalls and the warm grass upon which we had lain in the hidden cove.

Finally, with the sun high above, I dressed and made my way to the car. The world seemed a different place, the sky bluer, the grass greener, the sun brighter. Inside my groin lay a molten core filled with sensual energy.

Like a magical dragon, burning passion kept me awake at night with its intensity. I imagined my lover's fine hands playing musical scales on my ribs, teasing out the coiled desire I held so tightly within my innermost core. Now it refused to reassemble and lay there, inside me, awaiting the master tuner's return. When next I saw him, there was more than a rumble in my belly—I carried his child.

I returned to the cove as the moon reached her fullness, and just as I was about to give up, I saw him emerge from the water to begin his leisurely way to my waiting place. I could hardly wait for him to shed his skin. I rushed to strip to my own bare skin, longing to feel him close. Desire enveloped us both in our secret place under the trees until I screamed in ecstasy.

He stopped me with his mouth, holding me close until I returned to some sense of sanity. It was then his big hand rested on the soft mound of my belly and cupped the child nestled within. It was a caress both precious and tentative. My body roused to his touch and I clung to him.

"Must you leave again, my love?" I asked. "I carry your child and when you are gone, I will be alone. Can I not go with you?"

"Come with me?" He spoke with genuine concern in his voice. "If you leave this earthly plain, you can never return to it as I do. Are you ready for that? And what about our child—we know not whether he will be human or seal at birth. He may be a shape-changer; he may not."

"He?"

When my love left me that day I was unsettled, dissatisfied. I stayed in retreat at my place on the coast while the pregnancy advanced, had food and drink delivered by boat, and spent hours watching the water, hoping for his return. Only my doctor and the caretaker of the property knew of my condition, not that anyone cared, but I did. I could not let go of the vision of my love nor forget. Often, during the night, I felt him near me, deep in my heart, but this was a solitary journey.

Near the end of my waiting, I was huge and confined to bed on doctor's orders. A midwife from two counties away came for the lying-in. At long last, the day came for delivery, but when she delivered the big baby at sunrise and cut the cord, she cried out, backing away. "The

Lord help us—webbed fingers and toes! There be webbed fingers and toes—shall I get rid of it for you, lady?"

In horror, I grabbed for my child with all the fierceness of a mother bear and held him close to my breast. There, he rooted around and found the nipple already dripping with baby's first milk; then I looked at her in fury. "This is my child, not an *it*, and you will say nothing about him or the condition of his fingers and toes to a living soul. Do it and you will regret every word that comes out of your mouth for the rest of your life!" Never had I spoken words like that, and as they came from my mouth, I knew them to be a curse.

She saw the fury in my eyes and knew it for what it was. Chastened, the midwife backed away and began to clean the afterbirth. I could hear her muttering just under her breath and saw her make the sign as if to ward against evil, but she said nothing more. I had arranged for the cottage caretaker to send a visiting nurse to stay with me, and she arrived not long after the midwife finished her duties.

While she noticed the baby's fingers and toes, she said nothing, merely took him for a bath, helped me, and maintained professional courtesy.

A week later, my baby and I were on our own, and I took him down to the water to watch for my love for the first time. Tiny as he was, the touch of salt water thrilled him, and he laughed. It was a sound to gladden any mother's heart, and I held him close to my breast, grateful for this marvelous gift of life. Approaching my place, not more than a block from water's edge, I saw several cars parked nearby and smoke rising from the cottage.

Dancing around it was a rag-tag group of men and women, the midwife at their head. In her hand swung a long, wrinkled, and bloody cord—my child's life-cord. Quickly, I ducked into a grove of sea pine and scrub to watch their evil work, grateful not to have been home when they came.

With my child at the breast to keep him quiet, I made my way down to the inlet on foot, my heart filled with anger and sorrow. Approaching the shoreline, a familiar head rose from the water then swam toward us. With him were others—many sea people. When they emerged to follow him, all moved as one toward my cottage, stripped of their rich, dark skins of fur, naked, muscular, and unafraid.

Screams of surprise and fear soon rose in the distance. Rattletrap cars roared to life as the foolish villains fled. Lying on the porch was the midwife. Not dead, but disoriented, she was mute for the rest of her life and never again told the story of what she had seen. No one believed the others….

My love, his magnificent brethren surrounding us, stood in front of me, holding his baby and me. When he took the child, at first I feared his reaction, but then he said, "Ah, I see the webs on his fingers and toes—this child will adapt and shape-shift in both worlds." When he turned to me, I saw only love in his eyes. He would neither reject our child nor abandon me. "Are you ready for my world, my love?"

That day began an odyssey that continues to this day, as in the robes of a seal my love swept us into the water and down to his enchanted kingdom beneath the sea. Our son is powerful today with web-marked children on both land and in the sea, but we, his father and I, had no more children—needing none other than the two of us.

Slice of Life

We sit on sand
white as talcum—
close,
but not touching.

Lazy-making waves
tease without touching,
sand crystals cling to
crooked toes,
beads of sweat run down backs
hidden from sun's rays.

On the horizon a sailboat
changes course—
a sliver,
where once a white triangle
shone bright,
now gone.

The Ship's Lantern

From the day he hung the ship's lantern in her hallway, Ginny knew its meaning to be far more than a charming gift from the captain. To her, it spoke of love and his promise to return. To him, the lamp, visible far out in the bay, meant she waited still.

For nearly thirty years, she watched that ancient ship's light, keeping the wick trimmed and fresh oil ready for each night's lighting. Every evening, she waited for a man who never came—the lover who sailed away with the morning sun, mouthing sweet words on the wind that bore him to sea. This night, no light shown through the glass and she lay still, waiting for death's ghostly touch.

"I will love you forever, Ginny Lowe. Wait for me," he said. Wait she did, for there was no room in her heart, nor in her bed for another. Rich, chestnut hair turned gray and then white. Warm, green eyes grew dull; still, she waited.

At times, she felt him draw near in the netherworld of dreams, a tall man at the height of his powers when last she saw him, and she found herself surprised at the response she felt in the secret regions of her body. Old memories embedded there simmered still, ready to flame at his touch.

Ah, he wouldn't look at me now, she thought to herself. If he lives still, there's a wife and the children of his seed scattered far and wide, no doubt. Nevertheless, she waited, tending the lamp and dreaming of him almost every night.

They met when she was just past youth's first bloom, yet bursting with energy and robust health. Awaiting the arrival of a supply ship in the Apalachicola Bay, she whiled away the time with a light lunch of boiled shrimp, tangy sauce, and sweet iced tea. Bright sunlight flooded the dim room when the door opened, and a tall, sunburned man entered.

He scanned the room as if looking for someone. When he found her, green eyes locked with his blue. He walked straight to her, taking the seat next to hers without asking.

"Are you Miss Virginia Lowe?" he asked, with a sense of familiarity that told her he already knew who she was.

"Yes, I am," she responded with a hint of reserve in her voice. "Who, may I ask, are you?"

When he grinned, her virgin heart stopped in its tracks. She caught her breath quickly to hide the discomfort his nearness caused. He saw the blush bloom on her neck to flood the fair skin of her face, and he smiled even more broadly, easily reading her thoughts. She hated the betrayal of that blush, despising herself for it. In defiance, she arched her delicate brows and stared at him boldly, without apology.

"By all the gods of earth and sea, a woman who can still blush!" he exclaimed. Then he pushed his big hand into hers and introduced himself. "My name is Jackson, Miss Lowe, Henri Jackson." Pointing toward the Gulf of Mexico, he added, "I'm captain of that ship you see in the distance, at your service, ma'am."

"I'm pleased to make your acquaintance, Captain, but I fail to see why you have introduced yourself," she said, retrieving her hand with some effort. "Unless it is about the delivery of a small sailboat and some items I've ordered from the mainland. Have you brought them to me?"

"I must beg your pardon for rushing at you like that," he replied, pulling away just a fraction. "Yes, I've brought your boat, the supplies you ordered, and stores for some of your neighbors as well."

Before she could respond, he added, "I must say you've surprised me, ma'am."

"Captain, in what way, have I surprised you?" she responded with unexpected warmth. "It is I who should be surprised—I was awaiting a common sailor's announcement, not a visit from the captain himself."

"Ah, yes," said the big man, running a hand through thick, unruly sun-bleached hair. "I like these parts, having been here in the past. I had a yen for a sumptuous feast of fried oysters, shrimp, and scallops, so we anchored the ship, and I and two of my crew came ashore in your little boat." He picked up a menu and without pause added, "Shall we dine together? I'm famished."

At the abruptness of his invitation, Ginny drew back in surprise, standing down from her stool to the floor. "Thank you, no, Captain, I've just finished my lunch. If it won't inconvenience you too much, I'd like to see my boat if you please." She was startled to hear laughter around her as she left him sitting there, staring at her. She blushed, yet again, when the big man followed at her heels, towering over her small frame. She hated to be the center of attention, but there was little she could do about it. Ignoring the curious patrons, most of whom knew her quite well and were following the exchange with avid attention, she stiffened her spine and left the cool darkness of the seafood shack. He laughed when she squinted in Apalachicola's brilliant sunshine, moving to shield her from it with his big body.

"Please, Miss Lowe, let me apologize, for I believe I have offended you," he said as she walked briskly down to the docks. "Truly, I meant no offense and hope you can forgive my forwardness. I knew you to be waiting there for word about your boat, but I wasn't expecting a woman like you."

"And just what were you expecting, Captain?" she said hotly, turning around to face him. "A coarse fisherwoman dressed in overalls and white, rubber boots? I do have them, you know, anybody with a grain of sense would wear them for scalloping and oystering on the coast."

He sobered at the tone of her voice and responded, saying, "I'm not sure who or what I was expecting Miss Lowe, but it surely wasn't you." His words were nearly lost in quick gusts of wind from the water, but Ginny forgot everything when she saw the little sailboat docked in her private slip. It was just as she had ordered with a nicely sealed bottom, painted bright white with beautiful brass and mahogany appointments.

In her eagerness, and without another thought for the handsome captain, Ginny Lowe stepped into her boat, hoisted the sail, and pushed away, catching laughter in the wind as she went. The captain watched in astonishment as she tacked, rounded the bend of the estuary, and disappeared. He stood there staring, mouth agape, and then went back to the oyster shack for directions.

Ginny realized her rudeness as she approached the dock near the old Battery Park, secured the boat, and then made her way up to the house trying to think what to do. She could send a post with her appreciation of the captain to her factor with the next boat out, but secretly, she hoped to see him again.

Her heart swelled with pride as she approached the fine old Victorian home that commanded so much of her attention and money. Just to keep its soft, butter-yellow exterior and trim painted cost a small fortune. Well respected in the small Florida community, and sole heir to her father's riches, she lived alone with no one but a few orange tabby cats for company, and she enjoyed her independence. Having weathered numerous hurricanes and waterspouts over the years, she knew the fragility of life and accepted it; she spent her money and her life accordingly.

To her surprise, the captain rose as she approached the front porch. "I do hope you'll forgive my forwardness once again, ma'am, but there's the issue of payment. Might I wait out here while you get it?" he said in a dispassionate voice, handing her the invoice.

"Oh, my gracious—you haven't been paid? My factor on the mainland should have taken care of that on my behalf," she said, embarrassed. "Wait out here if you will, and I will bring some tea and your payment."

Satisfied, he settled back into the cushion of the deep-seated, wicker rocker with a slight grin. Looking around and liking what he saw, the sea captain waited patiently for Ginny's return. The verdant park across the street, furnished with its Civil War cannon, was a reminder of a troubled past, but all was calm and tranquil that day. Lulled by the cool shade of an old oak tree overhanging the porch, and the orange tabby cat nestled on his lap, he fell into a deep sleep.

Ginny peered at him through the wide, bay window before going out with the tea and saw that he was asleep. Henri Jackson was a big man with a hooked nose that might have been broken in his youth and a full, sensuous mouth she longed to kiss. Surprised at the feelings he awakened, she sat down in an effort to get herself under control.

This simply will not do, she thought, catching herself up. I am an independent woman of means, and I have no need for a man— especially a roving sea captain—in my life.

When she walked out to the porch, it was as a composed, mature woman in control of the situation. When he opened those sleepy, blue eyes and smiled, her pretensions fled, tumbling like a line of dominos. She nearly dropped the tea tray but was helped by his quick action.

"Do let me assist you, ma'am," he said, and with the deft movement of a dancer, he took the tray from her and set it down safely on the table in front of him. When she sat down rather too quickly, he noticed, but wisely refrained from mentioning it.

***

Now she lay in the bed where she and Henri Jackson last made love. Gradually losing the use of her legs to arthritis, the stairs grew impossible to navigate, so earlier in the year, she had the bed moved from the upstairs suite down to the front room next to the bay window. There, she spent hours watching the water for a distant ship that never appeared on the horizon. Each night, she lit the ship's lantern, its runes dancing in front of the fire to light his way home, and she dreamed of the years they shared until he came no more.

Lost at sea they said—his life forfeit to the trade he plied. He lived for the sea, and the sea took him at long last, leaving her to the vivid dreams that came almost every night. Memories of adventures at sea with him and his crew, nights of lovemaking on land and water, heated arguments and passionate reunions. She held it in her bosom and shared that life with no one, longing only for Captain Henri Jackson to take her with him when next he visited.

The night the lantern failed, there was no one to light it again; the woman who kept the house would not come until morning. In vain, she tried to move legs stilled with age, and then she heard him call. "Ginny!" The voice was distant—surely she was dreaming. "Ginny love—can you hear me?"

Yes, she could hear him. Yes, she tried to say, but the words failed to come. When the lantern began to glow, he called yet again, and the runes on the stained glass panels began to dance and throb with life.

"Dearest Ginny, it's time—come with me." She rose from her bed without effort, whole and filled with vibrant health, to behold him just outside the window. Henri had come to take her away at last, as she had known he would. She moved to the closed, bay window, passed through as though it were open to the night air, and joined her love. They vanished together in early morning's gray fog; the lantern grew dim.

Had anyone been listening, they might have heard laughter and the secret murmurings of two hearts united forever.

Note: Dot Jackson, Author of *Refuge*, inspired this story

Night Call

Strange harmonies pulsate late at night
under stars shimmering from above.

Leaves and needles rustle—
dark's creatures creep,
safe from sun's bright gaze.
Crickets, drawn by light,
line up outside my door
their chirruping constant
under rain's gentle fall.

My great orange tabby cat,
Veda,
useless as a bug catcher,
but good company nonetheless,
slumbers at my side,
twitching, meowing in his sleep,
dreaming about insects that got away.

Body weary, fingers tired,
eyes strained
I cannot quit.
Mind wide-awake…
ideas continue to flow,
until satisfied,
sleep comes
at sun's rising.

The Curse of Stinkbug Hollow

Not long ago, I bought a small house in the rural community of Stinkbug Hollow. I should have known better....

That little cottage was the house of my dreams—a charmer with warm, vanilla, clapboard siding, sage green window shutters on deep windows, and a red-tiled roof. Facing east was a wraparound porch that fronted a deep, bay window.

Visions of flower boxes, gardens, and birdfeeders filled me with delight, and I could hardly wait to move in. No sooner had I unpacked the first box than one of the neighbors appeared on the front step. Instead of a nice pie or jar of preserves, she carried a strange object held gingerly to her chest.

"Hello, dear," she said, stepping inside without invitation, eyes scanning my belongings which lay scattered about. "I'm Mary Agatha Mayo, your nearest neighbor, and I cannot tell you how pleased I am to have you. It's so hard to keep good people these days."

I watched her closely, fascinated by the huge eyes—à la Susan Sarandon—that filled her face with wonder as she spoke. She was almost regal—a lady's lady, all prim and proper, but she held onto that funny contraption as though it were a lifesaver. I began to wonder what was going on when she dropped the bomb that almost chased me away from my dream house.

"You know dear, we single women must stick together, don't you agree?" this said with a gentle flutter of the eyelashes, a look that probably caused many a male heart to leap when turned on them. "Your realtor told us you'd be coming down from New York. My, that's a long way for a woman to drive by herself, isn't it? Why did you choose us?"

Frankly, the questions were coming so rapid-fire that I hardly had time to answer before another landed. I almost missed the big one.

"…and you do know why the last family who owned this place left, don't you?" This said with an innocence that might have been disarming had she not had that danged box in her lap.

I decided it was a trap—the box, I mean, not her conversation. She was much too nice for that. "Did you notice the shield painted on your mailbox? We all have them, and it's a warning to all who wish to come here: this is the stinkbug capital of the world!"

The realtor certainly didn't mention this dubious distinction to me, and I hadn't given it a thought. *After all, communities get their names for all sorts of reasons, don't they*? I said to myself.

I asked as discreetly as possible, "Miss Mary, could you illuminate me on this? I had not heard of the stinkbug infestation until this very minute." I suddenly realized her manners were rubbing off on me and heard her voice in my own as I spoke.

"It's Mary Agatha, my dear," she responded with yet another sweep of those eyelashes and then continued. "That realtor was supposed to tell you about this house and its history. It's just not fair…. Well, I suppose the task falls to me. Some years ago, the first owner of this house heard that stinkbugs could eradicate those mustard-colored Chinese ladybugs, so he smuggled some into Fair Haven—once the name of our town. I really can't blame him as the ladybugs were into everything. They stopped up my vacuum cleaner and clogged the air ducts at my house. It was just awful, but the stinkbugs? They made friends with the ladybugs and now, we've got both. You know how it is, as with most things imported, those bugs escaped the confines of his garden shed and flourished. They flew out like storm troopers on a mission, and before we knew it, our town was host to stinkbugs in addition to ladybugs… you do know never to squash one, don't you? The smell is—oh—let's don't speak of it. Anyway, it seems those hard shields protect them from everything, and they have no natural enemies. Soon, folks began to move away to escape the infestation, taking the bugs to new locations. Those of us who were determined to stay were desperate and tried everything, but this is the only thing that has ever helped." She held the contraption up for inspection.

It was a simple invention made of heavy cardboard, a maze baited with a sticky substance at its center. At first, I was inclined to ignore her dire warning, but at just that moment, a droning buzz sounded near my ear. It stopped when an insect the size of my thumb made a clumsy crash landing near my teacup. Sure enough, there was a substantial shield on its back. My first response was to smack it, but Mary Agatha stopped me mid-air. Quickly, she stepped in with a tissue, captured the offending dive-bomber, and let it go outside my screen door.

"Why did you let it go?" I asked. "Won't it live to reproduce a thousand more?"

"Elizabeth, you must remain calm," she said in a soothing voice. "Panic will get you nowhere in this battle. We'll hang this trap by your door, and that dastardly bug will fly into it and bring others as well."

With that, she went to my porch, stood on my one outdoor chair, and suspended it from the ubiquitous fern hook. There it hung in all its primitive glory after she took her leave. I was not happy. It was not my idea of appropriate porch décor; it was also a death device, but the situation called for further study. The next morning, I took my coffee to the porch. Beneath the box were the hard shells of numerous stinkbugs, belly up. How did they get out, I wondered?

I swept the offensive hulls away and settled down to enjoy my morning's brew. Just as soon as I inhaled the rich aroma, a strange insect with infinitesimally small wings flitted down to my arm and bit me for no reason. What? It was a Chinese ladybug. That's when I dug into the boxes and retrieved my sage bundle. I took it all over the house in all four directions to snuff the evil influence I now perceived to be there. When I had to keep relighting it, something told me the situation went beyond stinkbugs and Chinese ladybugs. I now knew I was in that house for a reason.

***

I had been there many times in my dreams. The color beige overwhelmed me on my first visit but it wasn't bland—far from it, as this cottage had a good feeling to it, but it seemed as though someone had tried to blot it out. I knew my former husband had been there from telltale signs that never lie. A black power strip lay on the kitchen counter, overloaded with cords and too near the sink. Unplugging it from the wall with a sigh, I left the dream and awoke to the morning.

From that time on, I wondered about that house and knew that eventually, I would deal with it in real life.

On one dream-visitation, I found a cat in the living room. It was gray and black, had a small head, long ears, and a huge belly like something from a cartoon. When I reached down in greeting, it became a wiggly puppy, a spaniel in brown and white, then became a little boy with a large head, vacant eyes, long neck, and an enormous torso; his lower parts were undeveloped, and there he sat, looking up at me, helpless. I must take the child home, I thought, when a group of well-dressed people came for him. "Did you know he was here?" I asked.

They told me a man has an appointment every day at this time.

He is alone—where is the man, and how could he leave this child alone? Then I knew this child was a curiosity—a shape-shifter.

Another time I walked further into the house. It was a simple, shotgun cottage with a hallway dividing it into two long sections, running the length of the building side by side. At the end of one was a hidden room. There, I found color running rampant, soft cushions, and luxury befitting a sultan's palace. Leaving it, I turned to look once more and discovered the room was gone—gone as though it had never been.

Years later, I came across a house that reminded me of the one in the dream. It was time to move; I liked the area, even the eccentricity of the town's name, and so I bought it and moved in. On alert after Mary Agatha's visit, I began to search out the mystery. At night, I sometimes heard a cat's meow, a puppy's woof, or a child's cry. Scratches and footsteps in the attic sent me searching for intruders that didn't exist. What I found instead, was thousands of stinkbug shields and a child's rattle.

I soon came to appreciate Mary Agatha's stinkbug trap and maintained it carefully. It did nothing for the ladybugs, however, and that became the onus of an ongoing battle. In early fall, they bombarded the bay windows, and those that didn't make it into the house littered the porch floor. Inside they were in every nook and cranny. At night, I swept my bed and slept with my head under a blanket to protect my ears and nose from intrusion. Every day I burned the sage, and I'm convinced that ultimately that is what defeated the curse, for cursed it was.

One night I awoke, once again, to the sound of a child's cry. Using my phone's light app, I made my way through the dark house, determined to find the source. Approaching the backroom, I saw the outline of a door in the far wall. It wavered and rippled, but when I gripped the doorknob, it turned easily. Through the door I went and into another world—the one of my dream. There it was—the shape shifting cat/dog/child, and again, the power strip in the kitchen was overloaded and too close to the sink.

This time when the family came for the child, I went home with them to learn more about what was going on. They were very well dressed and their house was quite lovely on the outside, with a giant shield painted on the burgundy door, but inside was something else entirely. It was a shell of a house, shielded by its exterior. Largely unfinished with no drywall or plaster, the exterior seemed otherworldly and intense somehow. Once inside, there seemed to be too many people as though they were survivalists who feared discovery. Great columns of dried food and supplies of all kinds filled the rooms. In the garage was a glamorous, tufted, Hollywood bed dressed in white and blood red and in its midst, the strange child who was not human. In the dining room a player piano played the same song over and over. "Welcome to Stinkbug Hollow, Welcome to Stinkbug Hollow," on and on it went until finally I closed the lid. The keys went still and silence filled the rooms.

Nothing was as it seemed, and nothing was as it should be. Throughout all was the pervasive odor of the stinkbug.

I finally left that strange, dream house, leaving behind the playful puppy and those odd surreal people. It rippled before me when my eyes opened, not quite awake nor asleep. A bittersweet scent assailed my senses; beside the bed, my bundle of sage lay in ashes, the bedside table singed from the heat that consumed the herb. Something led me to the porch, but I knew what I would find there. Mary Agatha Mayo's stinkbug box lay on the floor, amidst thousands of stinkbug corpses and tiny yellow Chinese ladybugs. Wrapped in a voluminous yellow bathrobe, her hair wound tightly in pin curls, I could hear Mary Agatha before I saw her.

"Elizabeth, Elizabeth, what happened here last night? I woke to strange sounds, and when I looked out, your house was shimmering in blue light." Then she saw the mess on my porch floor and backed up, holding her robe close to her chest. "Oh, my. Oh, dear, what have you done?"

I told her about my waking dream and what had happened with the burned-out sage bundle; her big eyes got bigger and bigger with every word. I swear she began to shrivel up and then dissolve before my eyes underneath the yellow bathrobe. When it fell open, I saw a shield imprinted on her chest. Suddenly, everything fell into place like a key in a lock. She was the queen of Stinkbug Hollow and the box on my front porch was the incubator for her progeny. I had destroyed her habitat, her multitudinous offspring, and then demolished her kingdom.

The beautiful eyes drew down to dots; the brittle shield I could see on her chest grew and her limbs expanded, then exploded to join the husks lying on the floor. The queen of Stinkbug Hollow was no more.

Soon, my astonished neighbors joined me on the porch to sort out what had just happened to Mary Agatha Mayo. None had suspected she was the source of the stinkbugs plaguing our community.

Amidst all kinds of commentary from the neighbors, I became quite the celebrity, forced to tell and retell the story for all to hear. It was fun for a while, but I was glad to return to some semblance of normalcy.

After the publicity died down, the community renamed itself Doodlebug Hollow. Doodlebugs are harmless, amiable little bugs, yes? A roly-poly anyone?

Tempest

Great storm winds blew,
tormenting trees tethered
by grasping roots.
Snow-laden winds rampaged,
roaring in fury,
tearing, ripping, slicing
earth's fragile fabric—
limb, root, and vine
groaned in violent chorus,
their cries ignored.

Anger exhausted,
tempestuous winds die down.
Darkened tree trunks sprout mushrooms
in waterlogged bark,
new leaves grow
on pregnant red stems.
Geneses

Ice Palace at the Top of the World

When wizards, elves, and fairies still ruled the world of tall craggy mountains, fjords, and deep valleys, one of their number fell in love with a human princess.

The Ice Wizard lived alone in a tall tower, as all wizards must. From there, on the highest mountain of all, he surveyed his stark white domain day and night; at his side was an enormous white wolf. It was the wizard's task to hold the ice secure on top of the world, keeping earth in right balance, and that of the wolf to protect him on his solitary path.

Just below the tree line, in the land of the Midnight Sun lived a princess of rare beauty. It was she, Lisanne, who distracted the Ice Wizard, breaking centuries of isolation in a moment of desire. In long summers of endless light, she escaped her governess to ride alone on her sturdy Fjord pony, red hair flying loose in the wind. The fiery young woman, vibrant and filled with impetuous youth, distracted the Ice Wizard, melting his frozen heart. Discarding centuries of tradition, he determined to possess her. From that day forth, the Ice Wizard watched for her from his tower in the far north.

***

One day, while out on a solitary ride, she chanced to meet a handsome young man. He seated a fine white horse and rode with a white wolf at his side. Tall of stature and of regal bearing, he was surely a prince of noble heritage. He was so kind, so courteous, that she forgot to be afraid. Soon, she found him waiting for her, but only on days when she rode alone.

Inexperienced in the ways of the world, Lisanne found herself longing to see her prince more often, but wondered why it was, he never came to court. Who was he? Why did he never visit the palace or ask to meet her parents, the king and queen? Still, as someone under a spell, she rode out to meet him, forgetting her questions in his mesmerizing presence.

The Ice Wizard, having fallen deeply under her spell, now regretted his use of disguise. He feared her reaction should she ever see him as he truly was—a monstrously tall, cadaverous man who lived in total isolation in a tower at the top of the world.

On her 21st birthday and at last an adult, Lisanne was officially of marriageable age. As it was the time of endless light, the king and queen opened the palace and threw a celebration lasting many days. Suitors from far and wide came at all hours to woo the princess, but not the one she hoped to see—the tall man with ice-blue eyes, white-blond hair, and a ready smile.

Almost, just barely, in spite of the attention, gifts, and delights of coming of age, she was irritated. Where was he? As the party progressed, so did her displeasure.

Concerned, the king and queen noticed the flush on their daughter's fair skin and worried she was taking ill. No, she told them, it was exhaustion. In truth, she found herself in an unexpected quandary—it had finally occurred to her that if the prince did come, she could be in an extremely awkward position. Her parents knew nothing about him or their clandestine meetings. To acknowledge him would require an explanation.

The Ice Wizard found himself in a similar debate. He no longer wished to continue the deception he had used with the lovely Lisanne. Another part of him coveted her and wanted her, whatever it took to make it happen. The web of fate spun around them, growing tighter by the moment.

At noon on the last day of her birthday celebration, with the midsummer sun slowly rotating in its circuit above, the palace heralds announced the arrival of an important visitor. Lisanne watched in dismay as the prince, mounted on his magnificent, white Fjord horse, followed by the great, white wolf, approached the palace. Dressed in court clothing, a light mantle of white ermine flung across his shoulders, the rider surveyed the palace grounds and then looked up to see her watching him. He smiled, dismounted, and entered the palace sure of his welcome.

Summoned, Lisanne hesitated, trying to come up with a satisfying strategy before going down to greet him. Halfway there, she paused to calm herself. *Breathe deeply,* she thought. *This is what you have wanted, is it not?*

He was speaking with her parents, the king and queen, but at her entrance, the prince turned to greet her, a cool light in his crystalline eyes. In them she read, "Is this not what you wanted, my love? I have come."

Certain of Lisanne's response and without preamble, he turned to ask the king for her hand in marriage. Instead of the warm welcome he expected, he sensed coolness on the part of the king and queen, then was insulted when the king requested time to consider his suit. His credentials as Prince of the Frozen North were impeccable—they could not possibly know he was also the Ice Wizard. The wolf sensing his master's chagrin responded immediately—ears at attention, ridge fur raised, and tail down. A deep growl erupted from its throat as guards stood at attention, and the king rose to his feet.

Almost… just for the most brief and fleeting moment, Lisanne thought to move toward him. Then she saw something in her beloved's face, something that showed her, he was not the man she thought him to be. He was surely a prince, but there was something more, and it frightened her. In a sudden moment of clarity, she knew she would never marry him. In response, she moved to stand next to her parents, eyes cast down for once.

Deeply affronted by their response, the Ice Wizard turned to leave, saying to the king who stood resolute beside his daughter, "Perhaps I misunderstood your daughter's response to my suit, my lord. I thought she loved me as I do her." When Lisanne failed to speak or look up, he walked stiffly from the chamber, wolf at heel, mounted his horse, and galloped away in fury.

"What was that all about?" asked the king of his daughter. "Just how well do you know that man, Daughter, and if so, why did you not prepare us for his coming?"

It was then she confessed to having met him on her rides for some months, "But Father, something is different about him now, and I fear him. I cannot willingly marry that man."

In his wrath with both the prince and his daughter, the king ordered the gates barred. He then sent Lisanne to the top of her tower to ponder the situation she had created.

Fuming, the wizard rode until his horse was on the verge of collapse and the wolf's tongue hung loose. The Ice Wizard reined in to stare at the castle grounds and the palace tower in the distance. Long he sat astride the horse, attempting to salve his hurt and bitter anger. He should have known better. Suddenly, with cold determination, he lifted a long arm, pointed it straight at the tower from which Lisanne now watched him from afar, and cast a freezing spell on the palace and all its inhabitants.

A flash of brilliant, white light flew forth from his fingers. In that moment, every living thing in the palace, down to the smallest mouse in the cupboard, froze into solid blocks of ice, with the exception of the fickle princess, Lisanne. She found herself trapped at the top of her own tower, which was now composed entirely of translucent ice bricks.

In fury, the Ice Wizard rode back to his lone stronghold to brood. Why had he not simply taken the silly chit? Instead, neglecting his work, he had spent months wooing her. Well, it was over now, and they would all pay, especially Lisanne.

***

Lisanne could find no way down—the steps were gone and her tower's sides slick as glass, but she could see everything in the realm. Every surface in Lisanne's new world was transparent, from the blocks of the tower to the ceilings and floors—everything. In the great hall below, it grieved her to see her parents sitting on their thrones, encased in sparkling ice. She, with her bright red hair, green eyes, and fair skin, was the only spot of color for miles around. There was nothing she could do, and no one from whom she could seek help.

When the midnight sun fled the sky, the world she knew went darkly white and still, covered in thick, packed snow. All around, as far as she could see, the world lay frozen before her eyes.

She knew deep sorrow every time she glanced down into the hall and saw her mother and father in stasis, frozen to their thrones. She cried hot tears of anger and misery that changed nothing—how could she have known the prince's response would be like this? Why had she not seen through his disguise?

Long she stayed in her tower of ice. When he first came to her, bringing the necessities she required, she hardly knew how to respond. Gone was the handsome, romantic man with whom she had been infatuated.

Lisanne now knew him to be the mythic Ice Wizard of the Far North—a cold figure of immense authority and dignity. Now very cool in his manner, he brought gifts of food and warm clothing to his ice-bound captive—a polar bear cloak to match his, tall boots of reindeer leather lined in fur, and gloves, of course. While he treated her with every courtesy, he did not offer to set her free, nor did she ask him to, but everything in her life depended on his whim. She was his prisoner in every sense.

One day she sat in her window, longing for the sound of a bird or warm human voice when in the distance a dark spot appeared in the deep snow. No bigger than an ant, it was the first movement she had seen in the months of imprisonment. On it came, growing inch by inch until she could see it was a man and a donkey. Behind them was a wide swath of melting snow. Traces of green grass sprang up in their tracks and birds sang.

At last, a young man by the name of Gitano, leading a donkey loaded with sticks, drew near. Crossing the frozen moat, and there being no challenge to his entry, he stumbled through banked snowdrifts into the grounds of the castle. There, he was shocked to see it constructed solely of great blocks of ice, the inhabitants held in stasis, frozen in hoarfrost. He might have run had it not been for the feminine voice calling out so desperately.

There was no doubt in his mind that magic was at work in that place. Covered in hoarfrost, the palace inhabitants were as they had been the day the Ice Wizard cast his spell. It was eerily frightening. Cold wind whipped around buildings with high piercing shrieks; ice creaked and cracked, constantly settling. Sensing danger, Gitano wanted to leave, but the insistent voice calling from above commanded his attention.

The donkey saw her before the young man did. Following the direction of its long ears, he saw a young woman with long red hair, her vivid complexion in strong contrast to the absence of color around her.

Fearing he would leave, Lisanne stood in the window of the tower waving and calling down to him. He failed to understand a word she said, but he understood desperation when he heard it. He was doomed to failure—with no steps to climb that sleek, glassy surface, no rope, and no hooks; he could find no way to set the ravishing beauty free.

"I cannot get you out, my lady, but perhaps I can help by planting trees. Something has killed them all, and nature is out of balance in this place. If they grow and replenish the forest, perhaps the ice and snow will melt, and you'll be free," he called out.

Thinking he had surely lost his mind—planting those skinny sticks would *not* make the snow melt—she drew back into her tower. Maybe her fate was to wed the Ice Wizard after all. When she looked out again, Gitano was standing where he had been before, a handsome man with dark curly hair and a sturdy build, looking up at her. All around him and the donkey, ice was melting. Finally, hope bloomed in her breast. She gave consent for him to plant the trees where he saw fit. All that day Gitano and the donkey made their way around the palace courtyard, planting trees that would surely never sprout, and then beyond, outside the castle grounds. The next day, it was with a sad heart she watched them leave.

While he could see Lisanne in her icy tower, the Ice Wizard could not see everything at the top of the world all at once. He sensed change in the wind and sent the white wolf to see what was happening below the old tree line and at the palace. When the wolf returned with news of ice and snow melting, he saw the trees Gitano had planted. They were flourishing, the ice was melting, and much of the hoarfrost was gone. There was little he could do to stop what Gitano had begun; a different kind of spell was at work, and it was one against which he had no antidote—love freely given, asking nothing in return.

While his power was great, he could not hide the sun behind magical clouds forever. Seething, he watched the world's transformation from his tall tower on the high mountain. The trees Gitano planted came to life, sprouted, and began to grow tall. With the return of the midnight sun, and spring's chill warmth, the snow and ice continued to melt, and those held in bondage were set free. He fretted as they danced with joy at their delivery from bondage.

The Ice Wizard in his glacial tower on top of the highest mountain at the top of the world, watched in chagrin as Lisanne's tower of ice gently collapsed on itself. He clenched his teeth when the object of his fierce obsession walked free, a captive no more. She greeted her parents, now warm and vital, with much rejoicing.

As her world warmed with love, the Ice Wizard's own domain froze into a solid sheet of ice, imprisoning him and his minions forever. Water held in suspension, flowed down into rivers flowing south, and the frozen north renewed herself in right balance under the sun.

Still, there is one more person to consider in this story—Gitano. He never forgot the young woman who stole his heart at the top of the world. After replanting trees in all the places where they had gone extinct, and setting the earth to balance again, he and the donkey made their way north, ostensibly to see how well the earth had replenished herself in that cold, cold land.

Lichens covered the hills and valleys, ground-hugging arctic willow provided an understory, and sturdy forests of birch, stunted by the wind and cold, again flourished in their right place. On he went, following his heart, until he reached the place he remembered so well. There, he found a bustling community surrounding a fine palace. When he requested entry, the bridge was let down over a flowing moat of clear mountain water. When he entered the palace, a young woman with green eyes, red hair, an excellent memory, and a grateful heart made him welcome. It may well be, they live there still….

Ultimate Orgasm

A fiery, burning orb,
Father Sun cast his golden net
over sea's endless horizon,
each fine grain of sand
and gilded spider web a reflection of his glory.

But then that great, gaudy coral egg
sank out of sight,
consumed by Earth Mother,
eagerly seeking her dark, succulent nest.

Low-lying, lavender clouds
rimmed in rose-gold held their embrace
for a brief, roseate moment.

Sister Moon rose in her fullness.
Night's dark creatures danced wild and free,
black fingers against a cold silver screen.

Wind-baby sifted through twisted sea pines,
rustling russet marsh grasses,
tossing ghostly crystals in abandon.

Birds chanted ancient rhythms borne on rippling waves
sliding back and forth from shore
in sultry seduction.

Earth Mother, satiated,
awaited Father Sun's reawakening—
a temple... raw... primitive... eternal.

Laugh at the Moon No More

Rosalyn Rasmussen's mother died at her birth—a life for a life it seemed, leaving the tiny baby to its father and elder brother to raise. As she grew up, neither her father nor her brother understood the child's distance, lack of response, or her unusual reaction to the moon.

Their first intimation of a real problem with Rosalyn came when she was five. It was Halloween—time of the Harvest Moon; Rosalyn and her brother Bobby were returning from trick or treating accompanied by their father, and the family dog, Juno.

Rough waves crashed against ancient rock as they walked on a dark path near the seawall. Dressed in their trick or treat finery, bellies stuffed with candy, they danced along the footpath in the falling darkness, Rosalyn as a luminescent princess and her brother a scarecrow. Sea spray, leaping over the cliffs, threatened to drench them, but they loved the danger of it, squealing as they chased its effervescent trail. In response, sternly backed up by their father's admonitions, Juno planted himself firmly between his charges and the steep cliffs. What the valiant dog could not do was guard against the danger from above and the effect it had on Rosalyn.

It was an old family ritual—that of watching the golden orb's annual rise from the cliffs. The sun slid under the earth just as they settled on the rocks to watch the ancient mystery unfold.

From their vantage point, with nothing between them and the moonrise, the view was spectacular. When the golden arc winked on the horizon, bringing with it an air of expectation and mystery, the little girl gasped. Her father and brother thought nothing of it, as they were accustomed to Rosalyn's dramatic performances. That cavalier attitude changed as the huge, beaten, silver-gold orb ascended in the sky.

Before their eyes, a strange essence encased the child, bathing her in an ephemeral, shimmering silvery light. Juno, ever sensitive to all things Rosalyn, went berserk, trying to protect her from something he could only sense.

The flickering phenomenon stayed with her only a moment, but from then on, she grew increasingly distant from her father and sibling. Juno, her protector, became the child's constant companion and only confidant. From that day forward at the time of Harvest Moon, Rosalyn began to transform both physically and emotionally, growing ever more withdrawn each year. Most startling of all, her own naturally, pale blonde coloring turned to silver.

Everyone remarked on the changes. Her teachers went so far as to call her father in for a lecture on hair and skin care products. "She's too young," they said, accusing him of altering her appearance. He, however, was just as confused as they were and had no idea what was happening to his little daughter. Her doctors were baffled, too. They eventually decided monitoring the case was their best method of dealing with the unknown. No one had ever seen skin and hair change like hers in all of the medical histories—no matter the time of year. While they took copious notes, none had logical answers for the distraught father or the child's teachers.

Eight years later, her father was gone—dead far too young from a raging flu epidemic. Rosalyn, just beginning to experience the mystifying emergence of puberty, was exhibiting strange behaviors that had her brother, who had become her guardian, worried. She begged him to take her to the spot where that silvery web of moonlight first encased her. Since that strange night years earlier, fearing another incident, the family had avoided the path, but this time, when he resisted, she insisted. When Bobby gave in, it was with grave misgivings.

Rosalyn was subdued on the drive out to the wind-carved cliffs. When they arrived, distant caves, barely visible to the naked eye, beckoned from below. Waves crashing into hollow caves and coves echoed loud in the falling darkness.

She found the old footpath, walked to the cliff's edge, and sat down as they had in the past, long thin legs dangling over the edge. Juno, now old and frail, stayed close with Bobby on the other side.

Darkness, backlit with gold, cloaked the night with a sense of haunting mystery.

Still as a statue she sat, hands clenched; the pulse in her neck beating palpably as the wind whipped her fine hair like a rag mop. Her huge gray eyes lit up with fear and excitement when the full moon's arc showed on the horizon. Bathed in Harvest Moon's divine glory, Rosalyn seemed to hover in suspension before the moon's slow rise. Juno, ever aware of what was happening to his little mistress, whined softly.

Thunder rumbled in the distance, providing a backbeat to the gold and silver orb's ascension. Fierce black clouds roiled, edging it with a fringe of black lace. The ancient disc was huge—something mysterious from a different time and place, filling the sky with eerie, circular power amidst the storm's transient fury.

When lighting snaked across the sky and fiery fingers danced on the water, Bobby felt something horrible was about to happen. He spoke to his sister, but she failed to respond, her mind and spirit elsewhere; the moon had bathed her yet again in that eerie, hoary glow. It seemed to him her body had become an empty husk. Desperate, he dragged her away from the cliff's edge, leaving Juno to bark at the orb of hammered gold.

"We must get you home, Rosie, there's no time to waste." He should never have brought her out to the cliffs, but it was too late for regret. He feared now more for his sister's sanity than her safety.

Getting her shimmering, cold, and almost lifeless form toward the car was a struggle; with each step they took, the gale raged a brutal battle against his efforts. It seemed the elements sought to rip her from him. Determined, he struggled on, almost blinded by the molten light that penetrated the storm's wrath and the dead weight of his unresponsive sister. Juno barked wildly, fighting the unknown monster alone.

Rosalyn heard the dog as from a great distance. Drawn by an irresistible force without a name, fascinated by the frozen-gold surface of the moon's mysterious face, she had already gone too far. This time, there would be no return. The golden sky disc that fringed in whispers of black was a real entity now—one that called her by name. The mysterious glowing orb of fire and ice had finally taken complete hold of Rosalyn Rasmussen.

Her skin's luminescence and the fine platinum hair whipping around her face reminded Bobby of sparklers on the 4th of July, but there was nothing to celebrate here; something ghastly was happening. Without knowing how or why, he knew the rising moon's power was draining her life force.

Fierce winds cut around them like sharp knives bent on severing Rosalyn—a mere wraith of a girl, from her brother's arms. Suddenly, their peril became real to her, but only enough to feel some sense of responsibility for her brother's safety. Deeply touched by his attempts to protect her, she wanted to find a way to get him home before it was too late. Innate knowledge told her he could not accompany her on the coming journey.

Seeming to come to her senses, she forced life into stiffening legs to run with him, trying to get her brother to safety. With one last glance at her sky mistress, Rosalyn slid into the car, allowed Bobby to fasten the seatbelt, and then huddled close to the door, wrinkling her nose at Juno's wet-dog smell. She could not stop the strange stirring in her breast.

Anxious to get Rosalyn home, Bobby pulled onto the asphalt, wheels spinning, driving at top speed, leaving the white sands behind. Had he been looking at his sibling instead of the road, he might have seen the glazed look in her eye and the strange curl of her mouth, but he pushed on. The roiling tempest followed close behind, hurling threats of thunder and lightning from the heavens.

At home, brother and sister ran for shelter, but then Rosalyn seemed to stumble, and then stopped mid-step with a gasp. Bathed in a glistening sheen, she felt again that now-familiar, pulsating pressure in her chest; the blackened moon called to her beyond cloistering clouds, a place her brother could not go. Suddenly, with a strangled cry, she broke from him, running blindly into the face of the rainstorm.

"Rosie, no!" Bobby cried, but heedless of his call she ran from him, oblivious to the rain pelting down from a black sky or the lightning dancing all around her. Darkness swallowed her; Rosalyn was gone, with Juno in her wake.

Devastated, Bobby searched for her, calling out in the face of the storm. Finally, saddened by his failure to protect her from the demons that drove her to madness, he retreated to the house. The electricity and phones were out, and he was cold, hungry, and furious at something for which he had no name.

Flinging himself into action, he made the call to 911, found a flashlight, donned his rain cape, and then pressed his way back into the fray. Searching for hours, all he found was Juno, who came to him soaked and limping. Rosalyn Rasmussen was gone, disappearing without a trace. She was probably gone forever, swept away to that place which had called her, that place she had both feared and longed for all of her life.

Would he see his little sister again? Perhaps not.

***

Ravaging wings of wind dropped Rosalyn down near a system of singing caves far from the ones she knew. Afraid of the strange echoes, at first, she refused to enter. Finding an outcropping nearby, she crept under the overhang and waited. The tempest raged on just beyond her shelter, its fury competing with that of her beating heart. She was frightened by the compulsion that had driven her into the storm, and apprehensive. Her skin glistened platinum in the dim light, her hair white gold, and she could feel little response from her limbs. As the sun began its daily ascent, she found a cave nearby, crept in, found a ledge, eased her stiffening body onto it, and then slept the sleep of the dead.

When she awoke, disoriented and alone, hair of purest, white gold covered her body like a blanket. How long had she slept? Knowing Mother Moon's far-reaching, ice-cold fingers were coming for her, she wondered what would happen. Though she was frightened, she knew there would be no escape from her fate, nor did she wish to try; it was time.

When the first quicksilver threads snaked into the waiting darkness, some sense of humanity clung to her still. She cried out in fear of the unknown, "No, please, not yet." Heedless of her plea, on they came, slithering to where she waited. She clung to the living stone as though she might merge with it, but its surface remained solid and unyielding. Reed-thin ribbons of undulating quicksilver traced a streaming path to her feet. Nearly incoherent, she prayed for release to no god in particular, knowing none would answer.

49

A wolf howled in the distance, the sound bouncing off the cliffs to echo through the caves. She almost wished for quick death; perhaps that was the answer to this glorious torture, but then the first, ghostly finger touched her. She felt herself lifted, wrapped in silken cords colder than ice, spinning, spinning into the heart of the universe—a fork of spun lightning, to join the awaiting moon. She was Rosalyn Rasmussen no more.

***

Whirling through the atmosphere, Rosalyn felt the warm, rich, red blood in her veins turn to ice, her essence as pure as that of Mother Moon. Sweet relief from the limitations of her fleshly dwelling awakened something else within her. A feeling of empowerment, strength, and invulnerability filled her with inexplicable joy. She watched her skin complete its transition to platinum and felt her hair begin to shimmer in threads of quicksilver. Her time with Mother Moon would never find expression in words, but when she returned to the singing caves, she entered without fear; she was one with the goddess of the Moon, one of the living dead, a gleaming, silver statue that breathed and moved according to the moon's desire. Imbued with strange power, all who venerated the wraith-like vision she became, served her with both reverence and fear.

She dwelt there in darkness until the next Harvest Moon, aware, yet held in a state of suspension. It was then a lost woman, injured by a fall from the cliffs, dragged herself into the caves to die. Roused by sounds of pain and the vague taint of human blood, the statue's eyes opened, and it seemed to breathe.

Awakened by some force she could not understand, the woman looked up to see the statue in a recessed area of the stone. Had she been able to run, she would have; instead, she collapsed at the hoary statue's feet and kissed them. At that instant, she felt healing flow from a cold, silvery hand into her body. Broken limbs pieced themselves back together again, torn muscles and bruises healed. Restored, she ran from the cave to make her way down to the village, telling everyone what had happened. In very little time others found their way to the cave, and when the moon was in its golden fullness, miraculous healings took place at the feet of the magnificent, silver statue. They called it the

Silver Moon Maiden. As soon as the Harvest Moon waned, the cave's entrance disappeared and those who made the trek, following the torturous path, left disappointed.

***

Joseph arrived at the foot of the mountain at daybreak. It was the time of Harvest Moon, and he was there in service to his mistress, the Silver Moon Maiden, who had called him to her side. Once a year she spoke from the distant cave in the side of a tall, inhospitable mountain, granting healing to supplicants desperate for miracles.

This time, when Joseph climbed the mountain, it was to bring a dog descended from Juno, the Great Pyrenees of the Silver Moon Maiden's childhood. He had brought others to her—it was easy to find white dogs, but each time, she sent him out to search again.

In the distance, he saw a faint glow in the cave he sought. Eager to make his way toward it, he pushed the sure-footed beast at his side round and around the mountain, higher and ever nearer to the one he served. The air grew cold and clear. It was harder to breathe, but still he pushed on. Others had gone before him—those in service to the Silver Moon Maiden, as well as those seeking her healing powers, but his was a mission in response to her request.

Exhausted by the long climb, at last he found the mystic beauty awaiting his arrival. Alone in her stone chapel, she stood before him, a pale, living effigy of perfect purity. Diaphanous robes of silver touched with gold, draped cool, translucent skin. The hair on her fragile head shimmered platinum—almost white, flowing over thin, shapely shoulders to cascade down around delicate, bare feet—eternally young, forever perfect, and completely pure. Awakened by the Harvest Moon's rise, her eyes glowed like blackened silver from a stoked furnace. He felt the response to her chilly allure in his groin, coming unbidden. When she spoke, however, he felt his blood cool.

"Why have you come, faithless one?" she queried in a distant voice splintered with shards of ice.

For a moment, he stammered, always surprised at the way the object of his adoration addressed him. Bowing to the ground in deep obeisance, he said, "My Lady, I have brought that for which you asked."

She almost smiled—there was still a glimmer of humanity in her, as she spoke in her impeccably modulated voice, "Not another worthless hound from the streets, I hope."

Shaking his head, he pulled the heavy basket down, and then gingerly moved forward with his burden. Finally, he tipped the tightly woven basket at her feet, and out tumbled a snow-white puppy, stiff from its long ride. Shaking itself, fine, white fur fluffed out all over its thick body. Completely unafraid, the dog sat down next to the Silver Moon Maiden's feet; she turned to Joseph.

"Ah, the dog. You are certain this one is Juno's progeny?" Nodding, he lifted the furry bundle in his arms, looked her straight in the eye, and held the dog out to her. Melting just a fraction, she said, "Thank you, Joseph," gathering the shivering puppy to her icy breast. "Forgive my jest. You are the most faithful of all my servants. You and all whom you love are blessed this night of the Harvest Moon."

Bowing, his heart gladdened, he took his leave, pulling the donkey behind him, his pockets no more full than when he arrived. His heart, however, spilled over with reverence for the Silver Moon Maiden. She was the Healer, and it was she who had made his little son well. For her, he would do anything.

For a moment, the little dog and his new mistress stared at one another—he startled by her coldness, she unable to reach out to him with more than the tepid warmth of her barely beating heart. After coming to this forsaken place of eternal solitude, she had missed Juno—the dog of her childhood.

Some years back, Joseph, the bravest of her servants, ventured to tell her she needed company, beyond that of her supplicants.

"Ah, you think me lonely, do you? It is, indeed, a cold, hard place, but it is also the place of destiny. Perhaps, if I could but have a dog like the one from my youth, it might help me endure the isolation." That day began an odyssey for him: she wanted something he felt was impossible to obtain—a dog descended from the Great Pyrenees Juno. A man of few resources, but with intense loyalty, Joseph found himself searching pedigrees. He made inquiries near the town where the Silver Maiden lived, before her miraculous transformation.

Background checks, home inspections, and follow-ups eliminated all but a select few breeders. Eventually, Joseph's inquiries led him to Bobby, the Silver Moon Maiden's own brother.

Frail from illness and now housebound, Bobby raised the magnificent protectors, the Great Pyrenees, and they were all descended from Juno, his sister's beloved dog.

When Joseph showed up at his door taken aback by the man's shabby appearance, Bobby asked, "*You* want one of my dogs? Are you aware of what must be done to get one and how much they cost?"

When Joseph told him about the silvery maiden who healed many who came to her, and her desire for that kind of dog, something stirred in Bobby's memory. "Tell me, what is the healer's name?"

He had heard rumors about the Silver Moon Maiden, hiding in a distant mountain cave, but discounted it as superstition. Now, without knowing why, he was sure it was his sister, Rosalyn, gone for so many years. Perhaps finally, she was reaching out to him. Somehow, he doubted it, but if she wanted a puppy from Juno's line, it had to mean something.

***

Restless and still feeling the effect of yet another round of antibiotics, Bobby decided to find his sister. Using the registration information Joseph had provided, he set out on an odyssey of his own. When he made contact with Joseph about his desire to visit the Silver Maiden—ostensibly to check on the dog—it was Joseph's turn to be surprised. "But sir, the Silver Moon Maiden only sees people during the time of the Harvest Moon. The rest of the year, she is no more than a lifeless, silver statue. Besides, it is an arduous journey up to the cave—are you certain you can make it?"

Dismayed by this information, and dubious about his ability to survive the rigors of the trip, Bobby delayed his journey. When he finally set out, it was with the half-hope that his strange sister might be able to heal him. After weeks of preparation, he turned a deaf ear to the warnings of his doctors and left for New Mexico. Joseph met him at the airport, and together they began the trek to the Silver Moon Maiden's cave. The trip took all day, and at times, Joseph feared the man would fall off the donkey. It was far more difficult than either had thought, so much so that Joseph expected the man to die on the trail. Struggling to breathe and fighting weakened muscles, Bobby plugged on.

As they neared the honeycomb caves, a white blur rushed at them. It was White Moon, his sister's protector. The dog ran at the men, sharp teeth bared and exposed, a deep bark rumbling in the barrel chest, but when Bobby put out his hand and spoke, the giant dog slid to a stop. His sister's protector came forward, sniffing at the hand Bobby extended. Finally, both man and dog sat on the trail to commune. Joseph stood to the side, listening and watching with wonder. What was the connection between this man, the big white dog, and the Silver Moon Maiden?

Bobby was adamant about entering the caves on his own two feet. White Moon pressed hard against his side when they began the final ascent, and the man leaned against him, using the dog for stability. The moon was full, filling the sky with beaten gold and silver as they achieved the cliffs where the Silver Moon Maiden's cave laid waiting. Others had been there before him, leaving gifts of flowers and food for the Guardian, White Moon. Some had left healed, others limped away in disappointment, but all received a blessing for having seen the lustrous, eternal Silver Moon Maiden unbend, smile, and speak to their misery. For some, that was enough. For Bobby, when he saw what his beloved sister had become, it was heartbreak.

No longer his soft, gentle, and quirky sister Rosalyn, from childhood, this silvery being existed by the Harvest Moon's power. She was majestic and very tall, perfectly formed, a living statue that breathed as a mortal only one time a year—the time of the Harvest Moon.

When she heard them approach, it was as though she awoke from a deep sleep. White Moon pranced up to her, rubbing his head against her silken robes, thrilled to feel his mistress' touch. When the dog herded the pale man toward her, at first, she failed to recognize him, but then his voice stirred her to memory, "Rosalyn, it's me, Bobby."

"Bobby? Is that you, my brother? Why have you come to me?" Something in her voice and the way she stared in his direction told him her sight was limited. He drew closer.

"When this man came for White Moon, I followed up as I always do. That's when I suspected it was you and allowed the dog to go with him. Are you not glad to have me here? It has been many years since last we saw you."

When the Sister failed to respond, withdrawing again into stillness, Bobby worried that perhaps his journey had been in vain. He was in awe of her, hardly believing this cold effigy's heart had once pulsed with the red blood of life. He recalled the day she disappeared into the storm, the frantic search, and later, the overwhelming grief at her loss. This imposing being bore little resemblance to the Rosalyn he knew and remembered, beyond the big white dog's obvious affection.

"Come closer," she said in that cool, detached voice. When he drew near, she touched his forehead with a hand that was ice-cold, almost burning with chill; it was as though someone had placed dry ice on his face. As the sensation traveled through his body—through every pore—he tried to turn away, but found himself rooted to the cave's stone floor. There was no escape—bound by the Silvery Maiden, he could find no release. The Great Pyrenees whined and growled, looking up at his mistress, and then back to the man whose eyes were wide with surprise and fear.

When the Sister released him, Bobby collapsed at her feet, feeling like a sponge with no muscles and no bones. Hours later, when he rose, it was to find himself outside of the cave. He had no more pain. The Silver Moon Maiden, gleaming and cold, had moved back into the recesses, hidden in her cave. He gave thanks but received no reply. When he left, Bobby took an image with him of the Great Pyrenees curled at her feet, its tail thumping gently.

In her cold breast, the Sister rejoiced. She was able to share the only thing she had left to give her brother—healing. An icy, crystalline tear slid down her stony face.

Wrecking Ball

Abandoned,
stripped of all that made it a home,
a dilapidated old house awaits destruction.

Bare floors and empty walls
play host to ghosts drifting through in dead of night.
A homeless man finds shelter under its rotting roof
and cats urinate on crumbling foundations.

Who lived in that once-charming bungalow?
Children, who ran through its rooms in happy abandon,
their mother's calls gone unheeded.

Earth and sky bear witness of your imprint, old house.
In spring, when sleeping bulbs awaken,
pushing through newly laid sod,
and irises bloom—
they will remember—
and so, will I.

Intruder

Alone in her house,
kept company
by a cat and a mouse
forgotten by all,
dead to some,
she waited.

Alone she sat, bound to a rusted chair that rolled no more, waiting, hoping for Death. Sometimes she prayed for the end to come, but that grim specter stayed away. As life slowly dimmed and vacuous eyelids drooped, a strange, insidious cold set in. Nothing mattered anymore. A cat and mouse, both in varying stages of decomposition, lay at her feet; they no longer stank.

***

Almost there, crossing over… what is that, she thought. Sounds outside the house—someone was trying the back door… the knob gives way; a rush of icy wind swooshes ragged curtains. Heavy feet laid softly announce a man, tall and muscular. Furtive, he comes—pilfering scant belongings, violating her sacred passage.

Drawing back into awareness again, she listens, unmoving, as he searches. Had she felt like it, she might have smiled. What is of value to a dying woman in an abandoned house, stranded in a wheelchair with nobody to push it?

With the stealth of a dancer he moves, fingering rotted linens, lifting pots, stopping the maddening drip at the sink, *thank you, Jesus!* rattling pie tins against rust-stained porcelain.

57

Finding nothing there to take, he makes his way through to the bedroom. She can hear him breathing—he is afraid, but he continues to explore, opening drawers, pawing through meager possessions. Finally, he pauses in the front room, seeing first the dead cat and the mouse by the cold hearth. He sees thin feet bound in ragged, hot pink cotton shoes, thick stockings falling down over the tops, faded clothing, and the glint of gold embedded on a bony finger. Thinking her as dead as the cat and mouse, he reaches out.

Head averted lest the scent of death infect him, he lifts one cold hand to slide the ring off the unresponsive finger. Shivering at the howl of a wolf nearby, a quick intake of breath stops him.

Crusted eyelids flip open, and pale blue eyes impale his soul. "Who are you?" She spoke through stiffened lips, corrosion in the pipes of her throat, blurring the words. Before he can move, one emaciated hand grabs his, holding tight.

Petrified—his ruddy, red skin blanches white. Hazel eyes bulge from their sockets at the sound of that crackling voice and the touch of one he thought dead.

Hitting the front door in panic, cautious no more, he runs screaming into the freezing night, crying out in fear and shame.

**

Satisfied, the old woman left this earthly plain with a wry smirk on cracked lips, the gold ring on her finger, listening to the man's screams. The wolf howled again, and then there was silence.

Cloud Dancing

Clouds dance on tall buildings
sheathed in onyx—
an outdoor movie set against a wild blue sky,
filmed without script—
subject to wind's will.

Lovely silhouettes dance,
reflections caught in glossy glass—
cloud's illusion.

Sultry shadow fingers
graze lush green grass,
sensual movement caressing each blade.

Inside, one
watches cloud shadows
move over earth's curvature
seeing only that which is literal.

Ms. Ruby's Red Carpet

Following my divorce some years ago, I went house hunting. Thanks to my brother, I found a charming farmhouse surrounded by orchards and vast fields of yellow canola flowers. Located in the tiny hamlet of Hinson, north of Havana, a suburb of Tallahassee, Florida, the old house had a wraparound porch, beveled glass front door, deep windows, and huge rooms.

Out front were two gigantic camellia bushes of the Professor Sargent variety. In blooming season, blossoms composed of tightly layered petals littered the ground in deep pink froth. Wild asparagus grew in lacy profusion at the front steps; a pecan tree graced the western side with shade in summer and nuts in season. A scuppernong orchard stretched far out from the house, flanked by pear trees, flowering quince, and more pecan trees. Lavender morning glories bloomed of a morning. In the fall, each year we lived there, vivid coral hurricane lilies bloomed in the grass by the thousands.

It was love at first sight; from the very first day I saw that house, I wanted to live there, but before I could fully appreciate it, the house demanded something from me. I knew, on my first visit, what my priorities would be: remove the dirty, smelly, red carpet in the front room, clean everything from stem to stern, and paint every surface, in that order. Unfortunately, due to the quick sale of our family home in Tallahassee, my daughters and I had to move in before I began the job. Had I realized just how extensive a task it would be, I might not have taken it on, but houses can do that to a person.

We had been there for less than a week when the bizarre occurrences began. First, there came a scream from my eldest daughter's bedroom. It was Kitty, hollering at the top of her lungs, "Mama, there's an alligator in my room!" Mortified, I grabbed my trusty broom and charged like an admiral on a mission to save my child from the reptilian invader. I forged into the fray and found a tiny chameleon on the cannonball post of her bed. Knowing what would happen, I snatched it up by the tail, and of course, the little lizard separated from her appendage. Tailless, the lizard dropped from my hand to the floor and scurried to safety, while the girls leapt onto the bed. Neither had seen such a phenomenon and that entailed a lengthy explanation of lizards, tails, and such. By the time I was done with my story, both of my daughters wanted to find the little lizard and make a pretty apology. We named that lizard Lucille, and eventually she did come out to nibble at the gifts of bugs and veggies we left on the windowsill. Lucille became a member of our farm family and lived with us for quite some time.

Then there were the swallows that lived in the chimney. Walking through the living room, you'd hear the soft rustling of their wings and gentle murmurings. At times, I found the sounds comforting, but if you happened to be outside when they flew out to forage or were frightened, it was like a black tornado shooting out of the chimney. With our first winter coming on, I determined it was time to clean the fireplace and set up my andirons for a toasty fire. Removing the big piece of plywood covering the hearth, I discovered at least a foot and a half of bird guano in there—years of it.

My actions disturbed the fragile sensibilities of the swallows and they reacted with a violence it is difficult to describe. Instead of flying up and out of the chimney, they flew down the chimney, out through the hearth and into the house. In their fluttering excitement, they disturbed the ancient excrement that flew up into the air like black powder. It seemed as though thousands of agitated birds swarmed in there, and again, I took broom in hand and set out after the invaders. It took all afternoon, but after a time, peace prevailed.

That night, exhausted beyond endurance, I went to bed. I was just drifting off when I heard thinly veiled rustling overhead. It was rats—I just knew it was rats. I hate rats. When sleep claimed me, it was peopled by giant rats, enormous swallows, and lizards the size of dinosaurs. The next morning, Kristy, my youngest, climbed into the attic to assess the situation. She found a silver teaspoon, two WWII maps, and nothing else. There were no footprints, no paw prints, no scratches in the dust, no nothing, so she brought the maps and the spoon down to me. Ghosts are fond of teaspoons; I knew this from numerous ghost tales about missing spoons. The problem was serious enough that some restaurants kept their spoons under lock and key, so I figured that by removing the spoon, we would be safe now, but I was wrong.

Kristy soon named our ghost Annie, and we grew accustomed to the rustling sounds above. I, for one, figured a ghost far easier to live with than rats and let down my guard. That old house began to wrap itself around me as surely as a mother swaddles her child.

The day came, when both girls were away, that I decided to tear into that awful red carpet. It really was bad—years of wear and tobacco smoke had worn most of it to a rust-colored conglomeration of ugly. I wrapped my hair in a scarf, donned apron, and gloves, and tore into it with a vengeance. What happened next was a disaster—those synthetic fibers fell apart in my hands. Old carpet padding underneath, now exposed to the air, released yet another cloud of thick black dust into my house, setting off the brand new smoke alarm.

The alarm set off the chimney swallows who were flying into the walls of the chimney, trying to get out; I was colored gray from head to toe. I couldn't even begin to drag the heavy chunks of carpeting out of the house. Wrapping a kerchief around my face to protect my lungs, I must have been a comical sight.

Desperate, I rushed to the phone to call my brother who lived across the road. "Don," I pleaded, "can you come help me pull this carpet out? It's falling apart in my hands, the smoke alarm is going crazy with the dust, and I can't stop it or get the dust to settle."

My brother, a minister by calling, replied with maddening calm, "I can't do it right now, Sister. I'm working on my sermon for Sunday." *This was Thursday.* "You just rest for a while, and I'll send Matt over after supper." Poor, longsuffering Matt. Always delegated to help his ditsy Aunt Saundra, I could see his face already. "But Dad, I was just over there the other day, what does she want now?"

As there was no moving my brother, I left the doors open, plugged my ears with cotton balls and retired to my bedroom, trying to relax. That's when I heard the rustling overhead again. *Relax,* I told myself, *there's nothing up there.* But I knew there was. Little did I know it was Annie giving me warning.

I had just begun to relax when somebody knocked on the door. I leapt up, thinking it was Matt, only to find my front porch literally filled with strangers. "Ma'am, we want to talk to you for a while about the end of time—"

"No, thank you." Tired and impatient, I neglected good manners and interrupted when he continued, saying, "I have a church of my own, sir, and I'm not interested." When I turned to close the door, they were still there, heads bowed in prayer. Unrepentant, I peered through the window as they finally piled back into their big white van and rolled away. Upstairs, the rustling had died down and the swallows were simply cooing in the chimney. This time when I lay down, I fell sound asleep.

About 6:00 p.m., Matt drove over to help me load the frayed and shredded carpet into the pickup truck. "Did those people stop by your house—the ones in the white van?" I asked him.

"No ma'am. They don't stop by so much now they know Daddy is a preacher." He sounded so much like his father I wanted to slap him, but as I loved them both, I refrained. We loaded the carpet into the truck and took off for the quarters.

I must tell you my use of the term quarters, is strictly colloquial. Those cabins were there before the Civil War, they are there now, and they still call them quarters. I would expect they will stand long after I am gone. Both my house and the quarters were once part of a huge plantation property. Formerly, homes to slaves that worked the plantation, most of the little houses in the quarters still had no electricity and no running water when I moved into my house across the road. The ugly dumpster sat in the middle of the half-circle of their little community with the houses clustered around it. The residents had planted coleus, impatiens, gladiolas, hydrangeas, and roses around their houses, but there was no missing the centerpiece—that rusty dumpster.

We crossed the highway and took the tree-lined drive past the huge, crumbling chimney of the old burned-out plantation house, and on to the little neighborhood, clustered under a canopy of massive live-oak trees. Driving through the shaded tunnel, we could see people and dogs in the opening just beyond, but when we emerged, they were all gone. It was so quick that I wondered how they knew who was coming. Were they hiding from us, and if so, why?

"Where have the people gone, Matt? Are they afraid of us?" I asked, looking around at the empty circle drive where even the birds in the trees were silent. Shuttered, the windows were dark, like closed eyes. "But why? Last week when I was here, everyone was so friendly."

"Ah, Aunt Saundra, did you dump spray-paint cans in here last week?" This uttered with the unflappable calm that belies my nephew's fiery temperament.

Dread and foreboding seized me…. "Matt, I did, but they were empty!"

"Empty or not, they exploded like gunshot when Mr. Perry burned the trash this weekend. They thought it was an invasion of the KKK, with good reason. It's just a wonder nobody got shot."

Mortified by my stupidity, I was shamed, and impossibly embarrassed. Forgetting where I was—in the country—I had assumed someone came to remove the dumpster and took it away to empty the contents, not set fire to it! My thoughts, however, did not fix the situation, and I wanted to turn tail and go home. Matt, however, was determined to finish the job we had begun.

We were pulling the carpet out of the truck bed when a firm voice spoke near me, saying, "I'd like to have some of that carpet if you please."

I turned around to see a woman I'd noticed, walking by my place of a morning. She was a tall, black woman wearing a scarf tied around her head, gold hoops in her ears, and a simple dress. She wore no shoes on that warm day, but neither did I. Mr. Perry had told me her name was Ruby Tomkins. He called her a, "Damned uppity, black woman, puttin' on airs. She knows her place, and she ought to stay in it. Besides, she knew when she signed the lease there was no electricity or water to that house. She hadn't ort'a called the Health Department on me. It weren't her right."

His terse commentary piqued my imagination, and I began to fantasize about Ms. Ruby, but I would have had to run her down to stop the determined way in which she walked past my house. Confronted with the woman on her own turf, I responded, saying without thinking, "Ruby, you don't want this old carpet. It's dirty and smelly and it's falling apart." That's when I realized I had transgressed: as women of the South, we had not yet been introduced, and I had called her by her first name.

Realizing how forward I had been, I stuck out my hand and said, "Oh, I'm sorry—my name is Saundra Kelley. Call me Saundra, please."

She hesitated for just a second, then, looking me straight in the eye, took my hand and said with dignity, "My name is Ruby Tompkins. Most folks around here call me Ms. Ruby. You can call me that, too. Now, about that carpet, you let me decide what I'll use."

We talked on a bit and then found corner pieces of carpet that were still intact and clean enough to use. We took them over to her place, which looked to be a smaller version of mine. The bare living room floor, however, was riddled with huge termite runs, and that is why she wanted that carpet.

When we left her place, the living room was nice and cozy. Doors were open in the community, the shutters were up, and folks had again come out into the late afternoon sun. I left there, feeling as though I'd been given a reprieve and a measure of forgiveness.

That night, Annie's teaspoon went missing. We searched for it all over the kitchen and in our rooms, but the spoon was gone. On a hunch, Kristy climbed into the attic and found it exactly where it had been before. Again, the dust was undisturbed, and there were no prints of any kind, not even her own. The maps were still downstairs. So, what was Annie trying to say?

The next day, still confounded by the mystery of the traveling teaspoon, but eager to find what I hoped would be fine, old hardwood floors in my living room, I spent the day sweeping and mopping. What I found, much to my dismay, was a mismatched mess from years of patching with termite runs the size of my thumb all through it. Add to that, there was no subfloor—I could literally see the ground and everything under the house. With that discovery, I gave up and instead of refinishing a fine wooden floor, I spent a week caulking the runs, sanding, and painting—heresy to my way of thinking, but this was a rent for work job; I just had to make it presentable.

Ms. Ruby? She had a toasty warm house that winter thanks to her nice red carpet, while we nearly froze to death with those painted bare floors. I later learned that Ms. Ruby was a real change agent who had come there to help that little community move into the 21st century. By the time we moved away, every house in the quarters was painted. Each one had running water and electricity, and the offending dumpster was gone.

Just before we left that old house, the hurricane lilies bloomed again—thousands of them it seemed, and far more than I had ever seen before. I can still see them in my mind—a gentle meadow of soft coral, stretching as far as the eye could see. My daughters gathered up arms full of those fabulous lilies and we used every container in the house for them. Looking out over the fields, one could hardly tell we'd taken anything at all.

When we moved away, Kristy took Annie's teaspoon as a remembrance, and she still has it to this day. We never found an answer to that mystery, but I continue to wonder about Annie and the silver teaspoon. The old house is gone—removed to the ground for a sod farm—so perhaps our ghost found release that way. I hope the sod grass has memories and takes the hurricane lilies, yellow canola flowers, and morning glories to new homes the way my mind does. No matter where I live, that old house, the memories of it, and what I learned there, are nearby, always ready to spring forth in full bloom at my call.

Ignition

I am neither consumed with you,
nor by you.
On occasion we touch,
a spiritual melding of two like minds.

We are an awesome, fearful match
that threatens to ignite—
not to destroy,
but to bring life.

Fearful—yes,
threatening—yes,
for we are not an illusion
in which to cocoon.

Emerald Forest

I pulled off HWY 75 onto SR 319 to make the last leg of the trip home to Tallahassee. I always dread that part of the trip.

To some, the rural, gently rolling landscape is pleasing; to me, it is barren and overworked, bearing old scars and bad memories. Miles and miles of nothing but old houses, older cars, and bent people, all covered in dusty red clay, scraggly weeds fighting for life, trees drooping in the heat, and the ever-present dull, dry haze that chokes the very life out of it.

That day, in the distance, I saw an ephemeral explosion of red clay-dust stir up from the ground only to fall back to the earth. When it happened again, wind and dust swirled together to create form, no longer loose but now a spinning top, rushing toward the dry, old road I was driving on, propelled as though by magic. It gathered speed as it went, pulling more and more dust into the air, small at its base, spinning layers, growing wider and taller as it sped down the road toward me like a dust-filled tornado.

Hold tight, I told myself, *the demon is coming.* I gripped the wheel, my foot steady on the gas and readied for collision with that strange red-dust being—and collide we did. I drove straight into that spinning, swirling, dervish of abrasive wind, sand, and dust. When we met, the car jerked, temporarily thrown off its intention. A primitive sense of fear took me for a moment; the thing had an essence of life as I approached it. It looked for all the world like a reddened, gyrating, translucent, dust devil come to waylay me in that place of agony and brown land.

I had nearly lost control of the car as I passed through that maddened, swirling dust devil, but then I moved on, shaken but unharmed, my heart beating out of control.

68

I gathered my wits about me, thinking of other times when I came close to collision with the unknown, and passed through… like the day I went to the Emerald Forest.

***

At one time, I managed an antique shop in Havana, Florida, near my home. Situated within spitting distance of HWY 27 North, that store drew some strange characters through its doors, and George was one of them. He was a tall, skinny man, nice looking, and friendly, but not too much. Anyway, he particularly liked old farm gadgets, and we had a bunch of them hanging on the exposed, brick walls of the shop.

One day when he came in, we got to talking about the area, and he told me he had a place on a creek in the woods a couple of miles from my home. I passed it every day on the way to work and always wondered what was back there. He invited me to come see it, and I agreed to drive out the next day. The day dawned clear and warm, so I headed to the Emerald Forest as soon as I got off work. I had hoped to miss my brother, but it was not to be. He was mowing the lawn, surrounded by beagles and cocker spaniels that immediately recognized my car. Of course, I had to stop, and then I had to explain my business, which I didn't want to do.

Impatient as I was, I listened to my brother's diatribe and took off as soon as I could. His words followed me, "Sister, you can't be goin' back in them woods with a stranger man like that. We don't know nuthin' about him."

Something about his words got to me because as I drove further and further back into the woods and then off the road, I realized I didn't know that man from Adam's housecat. I was just curious and wanted to see what he had described to me, so I drove on, descending deeper into a stand of ancient trees the rich color of emerald green. Something felt strange to me in those woods, but still, I kept on driving. Finally, the track ended, and I stopped, got out of the car, and began to walk. It wasn't long before I saw the tiny, yellow trailer he had described and knew I had found the Emerald Forest.

It appeared I had picked up a drunk because when I got there, he was already pickled. He acted shy, which was good for me, and that put me somewhat at ease. He invited me into the little trailer, but I declined, preferring to take my chances with the poison ivy, which layered the ground in a rich carpet of dark green tri-cut leaves. Ancient, wild, grape vines draped the trees like giant reptiles, and thick, invasive kudzu cloaked them in dark, magical enchantments.

We were in a big bowl or depression, undoubtedly made by an ancient sinkhole, and I could hear a spring bubbling further up the creek. The Emerald Forest was deserving of its name, because that world was a fantasy of every shade of green imaginable, but it also seemed something had grown out of control in there. What was it that I felt in that forest? Primordial memories or present-day ghosts?

When George went inside to get another beer, I took my sandals off and wandered down the creek bed. I knew I should have turned around and left, but there was something about that place that held me in its sway. Birds sang overhead, and a male cardinal, red as blood, flew across my path, its brilliant plumage in strong contrast with the dense green. A doe, her soft liquid eyes unafraid, looked at me, sipped from the creek, and then disappeared into the trees.

I heard George approach before I saw him. He was walking behind me with a strange smile on his lips, a beer in one hand, and a long stick in the other.

"I thought you might like a walking stick, seein' as how you aim to keep walkin' in the water," he said. "Don't want a pretty lady like you to slip or nuthin'."

I thanked him, took the stick, and walked on. The cool water sloshing through my toes felt a nice contrast to the cloistering, moist heat of the forest. He followed close behind, but neither of us seemed to have much to say. Finally, George stopped and draped his long, lean frame on a log while I wandered further up the creek, seeking the mouth of the spring.

The sun began to set, and I turned around and began to make my way back along the creek bed. Up ahead, I could see him watching me, but something had changed—I knew it the minute he opened his mouth.

"You ever thought about how dangerous it might be to come back here with a stranger-man, girlie?" he said, his voice coercive and different from the soft one I had come to know.

I have to admit my heart raced when he said that, finding in the lazy sound of his voice new undertones redolent of menace and danger.

He stood up, as I got closer, looking me up and down, one hand in his pocket and the other propped on the tree; then he began to walk toward me in a slow, confident saunter.

I planted the stick in the sand in front of me and said, "Whatever you've got in mind, forget it because my brother knows I'm here." Looking up at him with a feigned air of innocence I continued, "You've heard of my brother—the pistol-packing Pentecostal preacher who lives in that red brick house with the dogs out on the highway? Didn't you read in the Havana Herald about him taking off after those vagrants that tried to break into my house? He keeps his spyglass trained on my place, and if anything happens, he's after them like a bolt of lightning." I cocked my head then and said, "It's a wonder he hasn't already come back here looking for me."

At that, he spat and said, "Holy shit, it's just my luck he's your brother. I'm outta here!" With that, he took off down the track ahead of me. One minute he was there, and the next he slid into the trees just like that doe had done.

Me? I breathed deeply and kept moving toward my car. I looked neither to the left nor to the right. I passed the yellow trailer, its door still hanging open, and then forced myself to walk steadily to my car. I was just leaving when I met my brother barreling down the track in his big black truck. Irritating as he can be, I was glad to see him.

"Sister, are you all right? I got the law comin'. I did some checkin' on that man, and we found out he raped a woman down in Jefferson County sometime back. He's been on the run ever since." He stopped to eye me under the big black Stetson. "Say, you look mighty pale to me. You sure you're okay?"

"I will be, Brother, I will be," and keeping my hands steady on the steering wheel, I drove home, angry red dust rising in the road behind me.

Iris Bound

Silken strips bind beauty striving to escape
attraction on demand.

Dust shimmers in sun's setting glow,
silken grids turned to gold.

Darkness falls as night's creatures
dance before moon's platinum orb,
weaving, sucking, slithering.

Sunrise awakens new magic—
spider webs sparkle with glistening dew,
a feast held in waiting for those who lived
through nighttime's dark journey.

Part II

SOUTHERN TOWNS AND ODD MEMORIES

The Legend of Tate's Hell, 1875

Once there was an angry man who lived on the edge of a great swamp.

When he and his young wife first migrated down from the Carolina's through Georgia, they found property on the Gulf of Mexico. Ignoring local lore about the swamp—no one had ever gone in there and emerged to tell the story—they settled down to raise a family. They cleared the land up to the edge of the peat bog lowland, built a cabin and a pen for their cattle, and left it at that.

Cebe Tate was excited when his wife got pregnant with their first child. He set about carving tiny toys, building a cradle, and he even bought a milk cow. The only midwife in the area was miles away, but he figured on bringing her early for the lying-in.

One night, Cebe's wife screamed out in the night—labor had begun, and he knew it was too early. He couldn't leave her to ride for the midwife, so the delivery was in his hands. He prepared as best he could, trying to calm his panicked wife while his own heart pounded in fear.

Suddenly, he heard an unearthly cough just outside the door. Panther! When light paws landed on the roof and began to pace near the chimney, Cebe's fear notched up a peg or two, and he began to focus his terror on the big cat.

The baby was breach and Cebe Tate had no idea what to do. His wife screamed, and the panther screamed in concert, over and over throughout the night, until at last she lay there exhausted from the battle she could not win. Still, the panther paced on the roof, coughing, and emitting that strange cry until at dawn, the woman drew her last breath and was still.

It was as though the great Florida panther knew the battle was over. Within minutes, it leapt down from the roof, and with one mighty jump, disappeared into the thick woods without a sound.

At daylight, Cebe laid his sweet wife out in her wedding dress and went out to dig the grave for her and the unborn child. Rage overwhelmed him at the site of panther tracks encircling the cabin, and he vowed then to kill the big cat.

Day by day, his anger grew as first one calf disappeared, then one of his dogs, then a young hog, always with the telltale tracks of the panther left behind.

One morning he walked out to find a path into the woods, made by the panther, dragging the cow away. In fury, he ran into the house, grabbed his gun, called the dogs, and followed the tracks into the swamp with nothing on his mind beyond killing the animal.

All day they tracked the panther until the hounds sounded the alarm at the base of a big, swamp red maple. Up in the fork of the tree hung what was left of the cow; on the ground below was just one panther track.

That night Cebe and his dogs slept in a TiTi Hammock where the white tail deer love to sleep in the day. The next morning, one of his dogs was gone, and he found panther tracks all around the hammock stand. Again, rage overcame reason, and he pushed forward deeper into the swamp.

The sun raged hot overhead, and thirst and hunger began to plague the man. His skin burned to a crisp, and his lips were so blistered they turned wrong side out and bled. At some point, he lost his hat—and that is when the battle was lost, but he didn't know and didn't care. Killing the panther was foremost in his mind.

By nightfall, he stumbled yet again into the stand of TiTi. By this time he had been in the swamp, on the savannah, up the pine hills, and down in the bog, tracking the elusive panther. Often, turning back, he could see the cat's paw prints crossing his own. Who was tracking whom?

The next morning, his dog was gone, and later that morning, so was his gun. Stumbling into the bog—a floating river of peat and jack-in-the pulpit plants—he lost his balance and almost lost his life in the bargain. Using his gun for leverage, he snagged a root to pull himself out, but it broke in half. Cebe watched as his gun slid out of sight, sinking into the muck.

An alligator, frightened from its den, shot up out of the peat, brushing him aside in its haste to escape. It was as though Cebe Tate saw his life down in the dark detritus of the swamp, but he couldn't give up. He had a panther to kill or he would die trying.

That night he crawled into a dry-bed cypress swamp. Praying no rain would come that night, he found a hollow cypress tree and painfully made his way over to it. Deciding to take shelter there, he took a parched palmetto frond and swept around in the tree's cavity to make sure there were no other occupants, and then he crawled in to die.

When the sun rose the next morning, Cebe took the first breath of the morning and tried to stretch. He had been in the swamp three days and three nights and was still alive.

What happened next is every camper's greatest fear: just as he opened his eyes, searing pain pierced his thigh. Gasping, he watched as a water moccasin leisurely made its way out to greet the sun.

Pulling himself out behind the snake, he knew this was the last day he would see the light. What he saw shocked him, as not forty feet away were the crashing waves of the Gulf. He had been in that mighty swamp for three days and escaped its clutches only to be snake bit!

The sun rose as he lay there in a stupor, trying to think. In the distance, a wavy figure approached. Seeing the bedraggled man lying in the sand, the hunter ran to him.

"Who are you, man?" said the hunter.

"My name's Cebe Tate, and I been in hell!" With that, an unrecognizable Cebe Tate fell back on his now, snow-white hair, and breathed his last.

In the distance, the panther screamed once more and then went silent.

That's the legend of Tate's Hell as I tell it.

Notes:

Artis Connell, my late mother's first cousin, told me about their great aunt, who was a midwife. It was said she delivered over 3,000 babies during the era of Cebe Tate's fury. She told the story about a panther screaming and pacing on the rooftop during an especially difficult delivery. There are many versions of this legend. This is the version known and told in my family.

Crone Am I

I've come to a stage in life
that all has to do with age
and a certain mindset.

At last free,
now Crone, Wise Woman
Me.

Beguiling sexual creature
I longed to be,
no longer on stage for all to
see.

Drawn
to hidden caves of spirit,
vast caverns I had no time to explore
in those frantic years of
before.

Child, wife, mother;
parents, husband, and lovers all gone
The last in line, my time is
Now.

I will grow my hair gray
and then whiter day by day,
sit and dream
and sometimes
scream.

I'll be an old woman
wise in my own way
I Am Me
Leave me Be.

Smooth Operator

Luanne Bugtussle hustled around her house like an angry wasp. It was the new preacher's first Sunday, and the ladies of the Missionary Society were providing a welcome dinner in his honor after the Sunday service.

Tiny and bird-like, Luanne looked as though she could blow away in the next storm, but her size belied the strength of will that lay beneath the frail exterior. She had selected a fine, fat hen from her own flock, killed it, and then prepared it for her specialty, chicken and dumplin's. The chicken cooked overnight in the crockpot and she had been up since dawn rolling the dumplin's for her masterpiece.

"He will never eat another mouthful of chicken and dumplin's without thinking of me," she said to herself, dropping perfectly formed bits of dough into the hot broth. "Why, there are people who would stoop so low as to buy a pre-cooked chicken at the grocery store and try to pass that off as real chicken, but not me—my dish will be made from scratch—every bit of it, and he'll eat it, and then he'll be all mine."

She hummed as she worked. "Amazing Grace" was the tune that most often came to her, and it ran in the back of her mind like elevator music. She figured that since she dedicated this meal to the man of God, she'd skip her morning devotions and get on with the preparations that gave her so much pleasure.

Luanne was a pillar of Cloud Level Primitive Baptist Church. As such, she fully expected her burial to be in the church graveyard with all of the saints gone by. By the time her poor Henry left this earthly plain, she was part and parcel of that body of believers, and could no more think of leaving the church than of marrying again. These truths, however, failed to stop her from admiring handsome men when they came her way, especially ministers, and dreaming sweet dreams of a night. She'd only seen the new preacher once, but that was enough to set her matronly heart aflutter.

Just two doors down, Annie Pearl Dalrymple was building her prize-winning, five-layer coconut cake. She knew well that Preacher Colson Davis was eagerly awaiting that cake because she had made sure to find out what kind of cake he favored. That it should be *her* specialty he desired, made perfect sense to her way of thinking.

A virtual mountain of white-flaked froth, Annie Pearl's cake always drew gasps of admiration when she presented it on special occasions; she had every reason to expect today would be no different. Normally, the rotund Annie Pearl licked the bowl as she went, but this time, licking the bowl seemed sacrilegious, so she set it down on the floor for Buster. The dog, a tiny Yorkshire terrier, was accustomed to such treats and nearly as plump as his mistress. He cleaned it up in no time. Satisfied with Buster's response, she gently put the heavy glass bowl into the sink to soak until she returned home from church. After baking and assembling the cake, she carefully frosted layer after layer, coating it with fresh coconut. She then pondered her work of art with a critical eye. Not quite satisfied, she added a bit more coconut with a quick flick of the wrist and pronounced the cake finished.

Everything she used in preparation was a treasure to Annie Pearl, from the bowl to the wooden mixing spoon to the pans in which she baked it. The metal pans were blackened with age—they were her mother's and almost as old as she was, but every cake she ever baked in them slid out like milk from a pitcher, and she had no desire for anything new.

She skipped Sunday school that morning, feeling the mission of feeding a minister of God to be a sacred service in itself. Taking her time after her bath, she sprinkled some talcum powder on her soft, rounded curves, and then she dressed in a prim, neatly pressed, white cotton blouse with her grandmother's cameo pinned at the neck, a long black skirt, practical low-heeled shoes, and dark stockings. Then, she twisted her scrap of thin, silver hair into a bun and anchored it with a flirty, black bow. Face powder dusted on her nose, she bit her lip and declared herself ready for church.

She pulled her big black purse—which could easily have qualified as carry-on luggage—off the kitchen table, went out the front door, and squeezed her bulk into the 1960 Ford Galaxy. Never married, Miss

Annie Pearl's prized possessions were Buster the Yorkie and that perfect, mint green car. The whitewall tires gave a little when she eased behind the big steering wheel, but the V-8 engine sprang to life when she cranked it, roaring with barely contained energy. She was halfway to the church when she realized she'd left the cake back at the house; she executed a hasty U-Turn and raced back to get it.

Luanne, meanwhile, dressed in a crisply starched, ice-blue shirtwaist tightly cinched at the waist, was carefully backing out of her driveway in an effort not to tip the huge pot of chicken and dumplin's onto the floorboard. She saw Annie Pearl rushing to the house and smiled in satisfaction. "I'll beat her to the church after all," she thought to herself. She settled the white straw, pillbox hat lower on her head, shifted the gears of her five-speed Dodge Dart with the expertise that was a part of Henry's legacy to her and barreled down the road toward the church.

Annie Pearl, for her part, ignored the sporty, white car as it darted down the road with her nemesis at the wheel. She got the cake into the car and gunned the big engine. The big car took the gas like a racehorse chomping at the bit, almost bucking in its eagerness to get on the road. The mint green car raced down the street, its owner's tiny foot barely touching the gas pedal.

Officer Max Eastonberry, the town's lone police officer, was eating his breakfast—a sausage biscuit and black coffee—in the squad car when he saw Luanne's white car streak past. Knowing it was Mrs. Bugtussle, and since there was no other traffic on the road, he let it go. Not five minutes later, Annie Pearl Dalrymple flew by in her big Ford Galaxy. The officer thought maybe something was up and followed the lady to the church at a respectful distance. By the time Annie Pearl pulled into the church parking lot, her face was red, her hair had escaped the bun, and the little bow was lopsided; she was out of breath, to be sure, but triumphant. The cake was intact.

Officer Eastonberry drew up next to the Ford, parking between Annie Pearl's car and Luanne Bugtussle's Dodge Dart. Noting her frazzled condition, he thought Annie Pearl was having a heart attack, and he called for an ambulance. For her part, when she saw the big, imposing man with his white hair and dark blue uniform looming above her, she thought she was about to get a traffic ticket for the first time in her life. Knowing she had broken the law in order to get to the church on time, she hyperventilated and passed out from the shock.

Meanwhile, Luanne watched the whole thing from the side door of the fellowship hall, a little grin on her pinched, elfin face. *Well, this is working out just fine*, she thought to herself. "Maybe they'll haul her off, and I won't have any competition today."

Luanne almost got her wish: Annie Pearl awoke in an ambulance and called out in a panic, "Where am I? Where are you taking me? I'm fine—I just got flustered when I thought Officer Max stopped me for speeding." She wrenched the oxygen mask from her face and demanded, "Get me back to that church, and I mean now! It's important—my cake's going to melt down in that hot car."

Spoken to in that manner by a lady allegedly in the throes of a heart attack, the ambulance driver reluctantly turned around and took her back to the church. The EMTs, however, refused to leave her side, fearing the worst. Annie Pearl's fair skin was flushed with excitement, her hair mussed, the bow was gone, and of all the horrors the cake was gone. Fortunately, the cake was safe and cool, sitting in a place of honor in the fellowship hall, watched over by the unflappable Max Eastonberry, a longtime admirer of Ms. Dalrymple. Seeing the look Luanne Bugtussle gave him when he brought it in from the car, he was on alert for subversion. Something was very wrong between those two. He knew it and was on guard.

Seeing the big man guarding her cake gave Annie Pearl a measure of comfort as she made her way over to him, fanning her ample bosom with a dainty white handkerchief.

"Why, thank you Officer Eastonberry," she said, straightening the bun and recovering the hair bow from her collar. Her soft, rounded face all sweetness, she said, "I'm so sorry I gave you such a fright, but when I saw you standin' there right beside my car, I thought I was going to break my historic record of no tickets in a lifetime. I wasn't having a heart attack; I was flustered."

The officer smiled down at the lady standing in front of him, her chest heaving, thinking she, for all the world, looked like a delicious apple dumpling. He said, "It's no problem at all, ma'am. I saw you drive by, and since Mrs. Bugtussle had just gone by in an awful hurry, I thought there was trouble up ahead, and I'm still not sure I was wrong," he said, tilting his head toward Luanne who was fussing over her pot of chicken and dumplin's and sending fierce, red-hot looks their direction.

Lowering her voice, Annie Pearl agreed with him. "She's always been the jealous sort, you know," she said, "and she's always felt she had to compete with me over everything; now with the new preacher, she's gone crazy with it. Now, I am not crazy over him, but just tryin' to do my Christian duty by providin' my very best coconut stack cake as a special welcome."

"I do understand, ma'am," he said with a gallant smile. "Would you mind if I come back for a piece of that cake after services?"

Pursing her little rosebud mouth, she fluttered her eyelashes at the big man, assuring him he could indeed have some of her cake and that she would save a piece just for him.

Folks in the church watched the exchange with interest. Annie Pearl Dalrymple and Luanne Bugtussle had been friendly enemies for years. When the new preacher, Colson Davis, auditioned for the job at the church and got it, the gloves came off, and it appeared there would be open war. To see Max Eastonberry siding with Annie Pearl threw an interesting element into the mix.

During the service, Luanne and Annie Pearl sat in their customary places on opposite sides of the small church. Each woman staunchly anchored the ends of their pews right next to the windows, in effect forcing everyone to either step over them or come down the center aisle. This pretty much left them their pews to themselves, which suited each woman just fine. At the beginning of the service, they exchanged glances and acid smiles before turning their attention to Preacher Davis.

He was an imposing figure with clear blue eyes, tanned skin, and a magnificent shock of artfully arranged black and silver hair brushed back from his forehead. A snow-white, long-sleeved shirt with cufflinks, an immaculate tie, a tailored, charcoal gray suit and soft, Italian shoes marked him as a well-dressed minister of the gospel. He was careful to look at both women as he preached, knowing already that his success in the new pulpit was to be dictated by their acceptance of him. Long accustomed to making allies and playing to audiences, he worked them with finely honed skills backed by years of experience. Near the back, however, sat the church secretary, Myra Ledbetter, and it was she who really had his attention.

Myra, a slim, attractive blonde divorcee who had been at the church about two years, had agreed to stay on as secretary to help keep things on an even keel until the new pastor arrived. When they met after his initial interview, she fell under his power immediately. From that first introduction, she would have given him anything he asked at the drop of a hat, and he knew it. He asked her to continue in the job if he was fortunate enough to get the pastorate. Looking deep into her eyes, he held her hand just a bit longer than was strictly necessary, noting the quick, pink flush that ran up her neck. He thought to bide his time and get the lay of the land before making a move on her, however. She was already in the can and would stay there until he was ready for her. Knowing he looked at her frequently during the sermon, Myra kept her eyes on the open Bible in her lap, a hot blush working its way up her neck. An uncommonly electrifying sense of damp warmth spread in certain very private parts of her body. The blush deepened as she felt it, but it was exciting to feel that way again, and she relished thoughts of those beautiful, expressive hands on her body.

Great power emanated from the Man of God that day, and Myra was far from the only woman in the church affected by it. Even the men admired his trim physique and ability to preach. Yes, things were off to a good start for the Reverend Colson Davis.

During dinner at the close of the service, Luanne and Annie Pearl sat on either side of the new preacher and maneuvered the conversation with an expertise he had seldom seen. Luanne's chicken and dumplin's were just as good as he had hoped; he made sure she knew he'd entertain the notion of having more at some time in the future should she wish to make them for him.

For dessert, he was able to get some chocolate pudding made by one of the other women, but it was about Annie Pearl Dalrymple's mountain of coconut cake that he fussed over. It really was good and definitely a favorite, so he could see food was going to be no problem with this flock. That the baker blushed as prettily as a teenager did when he complimented her made him want to laugh.

It really shouldn't be this easy to fool people, he thought to himself, never missing a beat as he used his magnetic power to subdue and lull the group into submission. He knew the rivalry between Luanne and Annie Pearl would be ridiculously easy to keep burning, and with any luck, their rivalry would keep the pious members of the church distracted enough to get the secretary under his sway, and hopefully, into bed. He had strong, sexual requirements, and they needed to be sated and soon, or he might get irritable. That would not do, not at all, as he intended to stay in this little church a long, long time.

Just before going to the parsonage to prepare for the evening sermon, he saw Myra leaving the office and flashed a smile her direction to let her know he knew she was there. Her heart missed a beat, but she nodded and quickly made her way to the car to avoid attention.

Unfortunately for Myra, both Annie Pearl and Luanne saw that shared smile, and both determined to eject Ms. Ledbetter from the scene as soon as possible. Annie Pearl, however, found herself diverted by Officer Eastonberry's arrival by her side. He had come to claim the piece of coconut cake she had saved for him.

"Officer Eastonberry, I do thank you for tryin' to come to my rescue today," she said, again looking up at him as he towered over her. "It's not often a knight will ride to the rescue of a lady in distress these days."

This time, it was his turn to blush, and Max Eastonberry returned her comment with one of his own. "I am a great admirer of yours, ma'am. Any time you need me, Miss Annie Pearl, I will be there. Just call and I will come. Will you remember that?"

"Of course, Officer," she looked down, almost confused by the attention. She took the big hand he offered in both of her soft little paws, saying, "I really do appreciate you, and it was good to get to know you a little better."

After eating his cake and accepting a big slice to take home, he walked her to the car, put the empty cake carrier on the passenger side, and helped her slide under the wheel. She drove home thinking about the officer instead of the new preacher, and it was Max Eastonberry's kind face she remembered when she went to sleep that night with Buster wrapped in her arms.

Tuesday, everything changed when she went in to get her hair done at Verna's Style Palace. Verna Snodgrass, town beautician and inveterate gossipmonger, mentioned the new preacher, the Reverend Colson Davis. She watched in the big mirror for Annie Pearl's reaction to the mention of his name

"I understand from Luanne Bugtussle that she took her famous chicken and dumplin's to the dinner yesterday. She said the new preacher just went on and on about 'em," she said.

"Is that so?" said Annie Pearl in a cool, disinterested voice. "I was there, and I didn't hear that. He was, however, highly complimentary of my five-layer coconut stack cake and asked if I made everything as good as that."

"Sounds like you two girls are going to get into it over that preacher," said Verna with a wicked gleam in her eye. "Are you sure he's worth it?"

Annie Pearl stared at the other woman in the mirror before she spoke. Verna knew everything in town and everybody, so she had to be careful, very careful.

"Verna, I'm not interested in that man beyond making sure he is comfortable and well-fed as the pastor of our church. Mark my words, Verna Snodgrass—there is no rivalry between Luanne Bugtussle and me. I will *not* participate in one, nor will I speak ill of her to you or to anyone else."

Stung but unrepentant, the hairdresser hid her smirk, turning around to get a new brush. Annie Pearl saw it and added, "Verna, I mean it. You keep out of this. It's folks like you, stirrin' up malicious gossip, which can turn something simple into a bonfire. Keep your thoughts to yourself, and we'll be okay."

While singed by that last comment, Verna was far from ready to accept defeat. She nodded and finished brushing the soft gray hair into its bun and turned the conversation elsewhere.

"Say, did you see the new shade of blonde I put on Myra Ledbetter's hair last week?" she said casually. "You know, she's real smart—too smart to be just a church secretary in my book. Such a waste, I say." Then she dropped the bomb she'd been holding onto, "By the way, I hear tell the new preacher has asked her to stay on as his secretary."

That was news to Annie Pearl, and she delicately raised her eyebrows in response. "Her work has been quite satisfactory as far as I know, Verna. I can't blame him for keeping someone who knows her way around the office already and has proven to be quite efficient." But Annie Pearl was seething inside. They should have gotten rid of that woman before the Reverend Colson Davis came to the church. There had been some rumors about her and the other preacher, but he had left before it turned into a scandal, and besides, she had to admit she rather liked the secretary. Still, she was potentially dangerous.

Wednesday, Luanne took her car for service at Leroy Grainger's garage. "You interested in selling this fine little car, ma'am?" he asked. "Seems to me like you'd want something less stressful to drive than this here five-speed. My son, Buck, just turned sixteen, and he would be mighty proud to drive this little beauty over the back roads and stuff."

"Leroy, you know this was my late husband's car, and I would never sell it, especially not to a sixteen-year-old who might drive it into the ground. Now, if you please, service my car; I will be back before noon to pick it up."

She sniffed, hung her white patent purse on her arm, and left Leroy standing there, mouth agape. *That woman is something else,* he thought to himself. "Sounded like she hated that poor man while he was alive— never had a good thing to say about him or his car, and now, she's all lovey-dovey about his memory. Now, don't that beat all?"

Joe, the mechanic, who had been listening to the exchange, grinned and said, "I'd be careful with that one, Leroy. Remember, we don't actually know what happened to her husband. I seem to remember that he up and disappeared, after a brief illness. Just gone. Do you remember a buryin'? I do not. Might be something stored in the trunk you'd rather not know about. That's all I got to say about it."

Grinning, they set to work on the old car, but Leroy couldn't forget Joe's comment. Maybe he'd better find another car for Buck.

***

Colson Davis, a wry expression on his face, laughed under his breath. Church folk were so easy to fool and it gave him a sense of power; their naiveté based on blind faith led him on. All it took was self-confidence, good looks, and the aura of a small boy in need of care. Since he had all of those assets at his command, his parishioners were fussing over him in no time at all, especially Luanne Bugtussle and Annie Pearl Dalrymple.

He figured the battle waging between those two old biddies would keep the church distracted for a good while, allowing him to pursue his real interest, the lovely church secretary, who was also the keeper of the books.

Myra Ledbetter was already heavily under his sway. She found herself inhaling his scent and leaning into him when he passed her desk or stood very close to her when they met in the hall. Oh, yes, he had her attention all right, and she knew it was a matter of time before he slid between the sheets at her place. When he did, she knew her legs would open to him like the petals of a rare flower. Already, she had given him the church gossip, even things she wasn't supposed to know. Of course, he knew how the treasury stood, and he had already taken charge of the checkbook, taking it from the church treasurer. This worried her for some reason, but all it took was a look from those intense, blue eyes, and her reservations melted away, leaving her panting like a schoolchild in his capable hands.

For his part, he knew this mark was in the bag; her blush when he complimented her hair, the way she straightened her skirt and held her legs close together when he pulled his chair close to hers made him want to laugh. It took all he could do to keep this courtship moving nice and slow, and it tortured him. The tension was building; he planned to bed Myra Ledbetter soon, and then to keep her enamored of him. He needed women, but he didn't want a wife—he still had one of those down in rural Bonifay, Florida. Thank God, he had escaped her clutches, and that she was clueless as to his whereabouts; he intended to keep it that way. Just thinking about her and her prying ways made him angry, the deep tan turning an ugly red against his crisp, snow-white collar.

Myra heard him coming down the passage way and quickly touched up her lipstick and mussed her hair. When he walked in the door, she was ready for him. While he didn't touch her at first, she felt his eyes take her in like a hungry wolf, and if he had moved on her then, she'd have laid him out on the floor right there in the church office. Instead, he walked over to her, laid his hand on her shoulder, and leaned down, inhaling her fragrance. Handsome and well spoken, the new preacher exuded a vibrant sexuality that she found appealing. It had been a long time since she'd been in a relationship, and she wasn't ready to dry up like those old ladies at the church, living on silly dreams. No, sir, she wanted the real thing, and Colson Davis was *it* for her.

"Um, what's that you're wearing?" he murmured, leaning close. "Is it something new?"

"Why, yes, Pastor, it is new," she said, feeling his breath on her bare skin. "Strange you should notice. Do you like it?"

Slowly, ever so slowly, his arm draped around her shoulder, and he kissed her on the neck. "Don't you think it's time you called me Colson?" he said. Her blood ran hot and cold at the same time and cut off her breath as he cupped a full breast in his hand. She just stood there waiting like a scared rabbit.

"What are you doing tonight, Myra?" he said, nuzzling her neck and causing the tiny hairs to stand up straight. "I'd love to come by for a few minutes. I'm lonely."

"To my house?" she said, a small squeak in her voice. "What if somebody sees us? You know this place—there are prying eyes everywhere."

"Yes, I mean to come to your house, Myra. Not to worry, I will park at the school and walk over, you know, getting my exercise…."

"Okay, shall I make you supper?"

"No, I just want some time with you."

This began a period in Myra Ledbetter's life that alternated between heaven and hell, sometimes in the same breath. The sex was so good she was dizzy from it. She found herself walking around in a cloud after each night spent in his arms, her legs aching with spent passion, then desperately afraid someone would find out and it would end in disaster. She was acutely aware of the scrutiny of Luanne Bugtussle, who had taken to dropping by the office at odd times.

"Colson, be careful," she said, playfully pushing him away one day as he sidled up against her. "I think Ms. Bugtussle is watching us—me in particular. I think she knows something and is looking for a way to trap me."

"Oh, don't worry about that old girl, Myra," he said, caressing her breast, slowly arousing her. "I can handle her." With that, they made their way into the office bathroom for a bit of play and relaxation before the Wednesday night services. When they emerged, the preacher looked invigorated, his secretary dazed and frazzled.

He had her where he wanted her now. Small slips with the budget would point straight to her, and to keep him happy, and herself out of jail, she'd keep her mouth shut. He was sure of it, and whistled as he made his way to the church office.

***

What he didn't know was that Luanne Bugtussle was an experienced amateur sleuth who stopped at nothing when she was on the scent. She swore she could smell Myra's new perfume on the preacher one day and she later told Verna when she got her hair done.

"You've got to be kidding," said Verna. "That brazen hussy… going after a man of God! Has she no pride and common decency? What are you going to do about it?"

"I'm going to expose her for a no-good, man-chasing slut, that's what! After we took her in and provided a job and housing when her husband left her, you'd think she'd be grateful, but no, she's got to have the pastor, too! You will never believe what I heard the other day…."

Nellie, Verna's assistant, heard every word and was concentrating so hard she nearly fell over her broom. *I've got to tell Buck,* she told herself as she swept up the hair under Luanne's chair. *I told him something was going on, but no, he wouldn't believe me. He will now!*

During Verna's smoke break, Nellie snuck out the back alley and made her way through the weeds to the garage. "Buck, Buck, are you there?"

"No, he ain't here, and you'd best get yourself right back over to that beauty shop and stay there, girl." It was Leroy, Buck's father, and he sounded like an angry hornet. "You've been keeping that boy distracted long enough. His grades is dropped, and he's plum good for nuthin' since you showed up. Now, leave him be. Get!"

That was a surprise. She had no idea anybody knew they had been together after school, least of all his father. She really liked Buck Grainger and didn't want to cause him any trouble. Her jubilant mood turned to ashes as she slumped and walked slowly back to the shop.

"What the hell is the matter with you, girl?" asked Verna when she came in the back door. "Get back to work, or I'll dock your pay this week."

Between Leroy Grainger's rough words and Verna's crude sass, Nellie crumbled and ran out of the shop crying.

91

Now, what caused her to act like that? thought Verna, dismayed by the girl's response. *I didn't really mean it.*

***

After the first flush of the affair dimmed, Myra began to recover her senses and took stock of the situation. It didn't look good; she was single—a divorced woman in a small town. The preacher wasn't what he was supposed to be, not by a long shot, and now she could see it. He was playing with the books and using the money to buy presents for her and clothes for him; she had no idea where it all went, but cash simply disappeared without an entry in the ledger.

Try as she would, however, she couldn't pull herself away from Colson Davis. His attraction for her was like that of a snake, and sometimes when they made love, she felt he was one. The ecstasy she felt in his arms overwhelmed her sense of right and wrong. Held by guilt and the need for secrecy, she was in his trap, enmeshed by passion, and above all, guilt. It *was* wrong, and she knew it, but she couldn't think what to do.

That week, Myra got her hair done as usual. Verna was busy sudsing her hair, asking ever more pointed questions. With her head in the soap bowl and Verna working her hair up into a lather of bubbles, her defenses were down. Out of the blue, the hairdresser mentioned Colson Davis. It was then that Myra knew the gig was up.

"So, what do you think of the new preacher? Some say you've gotten real close to him awful fast," said Verna, a wicked sound in her voice.

Startled by the question, Myra jumped. Verna jerked back, and Nellie giggled. Water shot straight down Myra's neck and all over her clothing and onto the floor.

Embarrassed, Verna spoke brusquely to the girl, "Stop that giggling right now, Nellie. Get the mop, and don't slide down while you do it." That advice was harder to take than it looked, and Nellie made the mess even worse with laughter she couldn't control.

Myra, at first shocked by Verna's audacity and her own dripping wet clothes, saw the humor in it, too, and began to laugh with Nellie. "Oh, don't worry about it, Verna," she said, and then looked at the beautician and added, "We all make mistakes."

She shook off the towel Verna was trying to dab her with, grabbed a dry one, and toweled her hair dry. She ran her fingers through it and left the shop with a wet head and sodden clothes.

Verna and Nellie watched as Myra passed Annie Pearl Dalrymple, who was on her way in to get her hair brushed out. The two women stopped to chat briefly, and Verna saw Annie Pearl reach into her purse and hand Myra something. She couldn't tell what it was and was anxious to know what kind of tie Annie Pearl might have with Myra.

Annie Pearl sailed into the shop with a pleasant expression on her round face. She was reluctant to engage in gossip that day, and only smiled when Verna and Nellie tried to tell her what happened before she arrived. "Well, she's right," said Annie Pearl, crossing her little hands over her girth, "We all make mistakes." That comment deflated Verna on the spot. Nellie snuck out to see if Buck was around again, risking being caught by his father.

Nellie knew she ought not to be out there angling after him, but he was so cute and had the biggest dreams of anybody she ever heard of. Besides, she had news!

"Nellie," called Verna. "You get back in here right this minute! We've got a customer a'settin' here, and this place is still a mess." Reluctantly, the girl turned around and made her way back to the shop, wondering where in the world Buck Grainger was, and why he hadn't come out when she called.

Annie Pearl sighed as Verna finished her hair. "You do such a good job, honey. I just don't know what this town did for a hairdresser before you came." She paid Verna and then turned to go. She stopped at the door and looking back over her shoulder said, "Yes, I do know what we did before you came. We washed and cut our own hair. Can you imagine that? I guess we could do it again, couldn't we?"

The last comment took Verna by surprise. What did Annie Pearl mean by saying that? Was she about to lose a valued customer? Suddenly she broke into an icy sweat and leaned back on the counter for support. She realized Nellie had given her the slip again and said, "Now, where is that worthless girl this time?"

Fortunately, Nellie slid in the back door as Luanne came in the front, her heels clicking on the linoleum floor. "Nellie, go down to Bloodworth's and get Ms. Bugtussle an iced Coke, girl, and be quick about it," said Verna, adding, "And don't forget the napkin."

No sooner had she walked out the door than Verna and Luanne were sitting close together, as Verna told her about the secretary's reaction to her questions and Annie Pearl's caustic comment.

"There's no doubt about it," said Luanne. "That blonde hussy is out to get him. We've got to stop it before it goes any further. They call us the weaker sex, but I don't buy it—not many men can resist that kind of a woman goin' after 'em, so we'll just have to take care of it for him. And don't you worry about Annie Pearl Dalrymple—she's not about to go back to fixin' her own hair—she'd miss too much if she did."

Nellie brought in the frosty, cold Coke neatly wrapped in a white napkin. Verna ignored her completely, but Luanne nodded absently and gave her a quarter for her trouble. She stayed just long enough to get her fringe shaped, and then she was off to set her plans in motion to save the church and the man of God from Hell and damnation.

However, Myra was ahead of her. An avenging angel, she let Colson Davis down hard when she found him in his office, resigned later that day, and moved her membership from Cloud Level Primitive Baptist to DePuy's Chapel across town. When he tried to intimidate her with his maneuvering of the books and the trail that led straight to her, she told him, "Go to hell, preacher man. You'll find lots of company there, but it won't be with me," and walked out without a glance at the handsome preacher.

"Now, that's a first," he said, admiring her spunk but already searching for a way to turn it to his advantage. He knew folk had noticed the bloom on Myra's face and had seen their glances—it had been hard not to touch her in public, but he resisted mightily, not wanting anything to interfere with his plans. Luanne saw those glances, too, but she took it as a personal affront.

"That man is old enough to be her father, and a man of God, to boot," she said to any and all who would listen. "It's purely scandalous; her behavior is, trying to turn a man like that away from the Good Book." Luanne quickly spread the seeds of unrest wherever she went. The membership was growing, but now some of it was purely out of curiosity—folks had heard about the good-looking, unmarried preacher, and the bleached-blonde church secretary who was about to bring about his downfall. In a small town without much entertainment, this was better than television.

***

Officer Eastonberry had taken to dropping by Ms. Annie Pearl's place of an afternoon when he got off duty. This had the effect of distracting her from the all-important work of watching after the new preacher, who wasn't quite so new anymore. The officer was a quiet and kind man who treated her with gentle consideration. Soon, Annie Pearl looked forward to his visits, going so far as to bake one of her famous, sour cream pound cakes so she'd have it on hand when he came by for a visit.

Luanne, of course, noticed the patrol car's frequent stops at the Dalrymple abode and put that little bit of information away for future use. When he drove up that afternoon, she barely noticed. After all, it was Wednesday night, and she had to get ready for church. Before she went into the bedroom to change, she stopped by the freezer and gave it a pat, murmured something under her breath and went into the room with a smile on her face.

It was something of a surprise to see the tall officer accompany Annie Pearl to church later that evening. She barely came up to his chest, but it was obvious she was pleased to have him there as her guest, and they seemed quite comfortable sitting together on her personal pew.

Preacher Colson Davis, however, was not pleased. The last thing he wanted was an officer of the law snooping around his church. He wanted no interference, especially now that Myra had flown the coop, carrying his secrets with her. He already missed Myra's company and her help, but had noticed Verna, the beautician, had nice legs. Even though she was a bit brassy, he thought she might be receptive to his advances.

The day Reverend Colson Davis went into Verna's shop to get his haircut, she almost passed out; her heart beat so fast she was sure he could see it through her blouse, and he was definitely looking *there*. Not only was he devastatingly handsome, but the way he looked at her made her dizzy, to be sure. She was afraid to put the scissors to that magnificent mane of black and silver hair, but she managed. By the time she was done, he could have disrobed her there in the shop with the window shade up for all to see had he wanted to, which he did not.

95

He thought little Nellie looked fresher and a much more malleable subject for his next conquest. The soft, pink on her young skin was from Buck Grainger's kisses out in the alleyway, but in his arrogance, it was all for him.

***

With Myra finally out of the picture, Luanne volunteered to help the preacher in the church office. It was something he dreaded, and he tried to avoid her, but his ploys to get her into his camp had worked too well. The attention grew irksome in the extreme. He'd barely get in the door of a morning when the Dodge Dart would pull into the parking lot, coming to rest beside his imposing big, black Mercury, and its owner would mince her way in bearing gifts of teacakes and chocolate chip cookies. It took all he could do to remain civil and flattering to the woman. All he wanted was to boot her nosy self out of the office so he could have some peace and quiet.

Not that it would have done any good to be rude to her—she'd have found a way to excuse it, and he knew it. Lest he made her turn against him, and that wasn't a prospect he relished at all, Luanne wasn't going anywhere fast—unless it was to the grave. Besides, he enjoyed the sumptuous cookies and cakes she brought. Maybe it was time to step up the rivalry between her and Annie Pearl Dalrymple. That might distract her for a while and give him some breathing space. Sighing, he ate another macadamia nut cookie and gazed down at his protruding belly. He was going to have to get more exercise, and soon, or he'd have to buy a new wardrobe.

***

What the preacher had failed to consider as he pondered his affairs with the church secretary was the kindness Annie Pearl had extended to Myra Ledbetter over the years. Even though she was profoundly irritated with the younger woman over her alleged affair with the preacher she still liked her, and wasn't in the least surprised when Myra came by one evening.

"I know you probably don't want to have anything to do with me, but Ms. Annie Pearl, may I come in and talk with you? I've got to talk to somebody I can trust." Myra looked bedraggled with purple circles rimming her eyes and dark roots that pushed up through the honey blonde curls.

Annie Pearl welcomed her warmly saying, "I knew you'd come by sooner or later, Dearie. Come on into the kitchen and have a seat by the window. We'll have a cup of tea, and you can tell me all about it."

Relieved, Myra shed her coat and followed Annie Pearl into the inviting kitchen. She sat down at the table with a sigh, which Annie Pearl heard, but ignored for the time being. She knew something was dreadfully wrong already, or Myra Ledbetter would not have come to her.

When the kettle whistled, she made the tea and let it steep. Conversation was desultory at first, but Myra gasped when Annie Pearl brought out her Blue Ridge Pottery cups and saucers accompanied by lovely, cloth napkins. She smiled happily for a moment when she found herself served a fine piece of moist pound cake. After they finished and their cups were nestled neatly in their saucers, Buster begged for Myra's lap. When she took him in her arms, the tears began to fall. The little dog swished round and around on her lap until he was comfortable and let her absent-mindedly smooth his shiny, gray and tan fur.

Annie Pearl bided her time and let Buster work his magic. She knew Myra would spill the story when she was ready, and so she did. Myra told her about the affair with Preacher Davis and her *coming to Jesus* moment at the beauty shop. She told Annie Pearl how she had gone straight to the church and resigned in her wet hair and clothes. When Myra spoke about the preacher's maneuvering of the books, Annie Pearl's expression grew stern.

"You mean to tell me you actually believe he came onto you so he could get at the Lord's money?" she asked.

"I'm as sure of it as I'm sitting here, Ms. Annie Pearl," said Myra, dabbing her eyes. "Well, maybe not all of it, he's a smooth operator, that's for sure. It's just that he's fixed it so the trail points straight at me, and I'm scared half to death. What if I go to jail?"

"Not over my dead body you won't, Sugar," said Annie Pearl. "I've been suspecting something was wrong with that preacher for a couple of months now, and this is the proof I needed. We'll get that fancy buzzard behind bars or my name ain't Annie Pearl Dalrymple!" With that, she picked up the phone and called Officer Eastonberry.

"Max, can you come over here right now?" she said, nodding into the receiver. "Yes, it is a matter of the law, although you know you are always welcome in my home." She hung up with a small smile on her face and Myra exclaimed, "You've got a boyfriend, Ms. Annie Pearl! I'm sorry, my preoccupation with Colson Davis and those damned books kept me from noticing. Congratulations!"

The two women were still talking about Officer Eastonberry when he knocked on the back door and came in as if he did it every day. He put some coffee on to perk and sitting down at the table, ate a piece of cake while Annie Pearl and Myra filled him in on Preacher Colson's illicit activities.

"Well, I can't say I'm all that surprised," he said. "I started pickin' around in order to see if he was on the level, and just this afternoon I got word from Florida that Davis is a married father of three. He left his wife and children several years ago and has been picking churches clean ever since."

"Well, I'll be flummoxed!" said Annie Pearl. "I knew it was bad, but this is worse than I ever thought it would be. He didn't strike me as being that kind of man. Vain, maybe, but I did not see him as a liar, thief, womanizer, and deserter of his wife and children! Now, what should we do?"

"I know what I've got to do, and that's to get a search warrant, but first, let's think this thing over for a minute or two before we do anything rash."

Annie Pearl noticed Myra looked a little pale and asked if she needed anything.

"No… well, yes… maybe a pregnancy test. I missed my period this month for the first time in years, and I'm sick at my stomach." With that, she ran to the bathroom, leaving Annie Pearl and Officer Eastonberry with their mouths agape.

Annie Pearl groaned, "Oh, Lordy, this is all we need, a baby thrown into the mix."

Max looked at her and said, "No, if we play it right, this may fall right into our hands. No, no, not the baby, Annie Pearl, this *situation!* It is ideal for laying a trap for the Reverend Colson Davis." When Myra returned to the room, he told them what he was planning and added, "Are you two game for this? Are you with me?" He didn't have to ask.

***

Loganton was a small backwater town. It was so far back in the woods that they still had a local telephone operator, Imogene Brown. She was born there and never left it in all of her fifty-seven years. She proved to be an eager accomplice when Luanne set her tentacles out for Preacher Davis.

"Luanne, it's Imogene, and I've got something to tell you that won't sit on my tongue another minute. It's about that preacher, Reverend Davis."

Luanne groaned inwardly when she heard those words, but she knew she had to hear it all. "Okay, Imogene, spill it. What have you heard?"

"Well, Officer Eastonberry put in a call down to Florida this afternoon, and I just happened to listen in," she said, her asthmatic voice reedy with excitement. "Preacher Davis is married! He's got a wife and three children down in a place called Bonifay, Florida. Can you believe it?"

That did it. Luanne's infatuation with Preacher Davis was finally over. Once she realized he had played them all for fools, she took it personally, and in some ways, it was worse than when Henry tried to run out on her.

A man of God should be a saint, walking in earthly shoes with the hand of God, guiding his every step, she thought. Why did he have to come here? Surely, he could have resisted the sins of the flesh had he listened to God, but no, she fumed to herself, he listened to that harlot and took the whole church down with him. They say Hell hath no fury like a woman scorned. You just wait and see, Preacher man!

She got the wife's name and number from Imogene, and put in a call to Bonifay, Florida. "Mrs. Davis? This is Luanne Bugtussle from Loganton, Tennessee. Yes, ma'am, I know you spoke to Officer Eastonberry this afternoon, but I have a proposal for you. Would it inconvenience you too much to catch a bus this afternoon, if I wire you the money?"

Madge Davis was more than willing to cooperate with the law and the pious Mrs. Luanne Bugtussle. The life she had lived with Colson Davis had many incredible highs, but the lows were a cesspool of misery. On top of that, he had left her and the children in poverty, dependent on the church he had taken for a ride. Perhaps this would enable her to recapture an element of pride again, while bringing her errant husband to justice. That very afternoon she collected the money at the Western Union office, bought a bus ticket for Loganton, Tennessee, and went home to arrange childcare for her three children.

An hour later, she was on the bus for the two-day trip north, waving a tearful goodbye to her children with an eagerness she'd not felt in many a year. It was time to bring the Man of God down, and with any luck, she was going to be a big part of his fall.

Later that week, Myra called Preacher Davis at his office from Annie Pearl's house, saying, "Colson? Yes, it's me, Myra... no, I'm not coming back!" she said. "Listen to me, Colson, I think I'm pregnant. If I am, it's your baby I'm carrying, and I'm going to need your help with it."

"What? A baby—there's no way in hell I'm going to help you with it." He yelled into the phone. "You're too old to get pregnant! And why didn't you use protection, you stupid bitch?"

Stunned, she listened as he ranted into the phone, supported by Annie Pearl and Officer Eastonberry, whose face was grave.

Gathering her wits, she told him, "Colson, if I am pregnant, I'm going to have an abortion—you are right, I am too old for this, but you'll have to pay for it since it's your baby, too. I can't afford to keep it, nor can I afford to end the pregnancy now that I am unemployed. I've got an appointment at the Women's Clinic in Nashville next week, but I'm not going to do this alone—you'll have to be there." When he started to argue, she said quickly, "Shut up, Colson Davis! Meet me at the clinic on South Main Street next Monday at ten in the morning, money in hand, or I will stand up in the church and tell the congregation all about what you have done, and I mean all of it."

Anger filled every pore of his body as beads of moisture formed on his fine forehead, and sweat stained the starched shirt he wore. When he cursed Myra again, it was with such a creative vigor and vehemence it shocked her to the core, but Davis finally agreed to the plan and hung up on her.

Exhausted by the emotional rollercoaster she was riding, Myra lay back on the sofa with a pillow held tightly across her stomach and chest, crying hot tears that seemed to have no end.

Annie Pearl, her sympathies aroused by Myra's obvious distress, washed her face with a soft, damp washcloth and plied her with hot blueberry tea. When Myra finally cried it all out, she lay asleep in the darkened living room while Annie Pearl and Max Eastonberry finalized their plans for entrapping Colson Davis in his own mud-pit.

When Monday came, Max Eastonberry assured Myra he would be nearby at all times but to take no chances. "This man is bad news, Myra; there's no record of violent behavior that I can find, but he might be a loose cannon when he's afraid, and this time, he's very afraid."

Davis was in Nashville as agreed, waiting for her at the clinic. She'd never seen him dressed so casually—worn jeans and running shoes, a flannel shirt and a battered FSU baseball cap pulled down low over his eyes.

"What's the matter, Colson?" she said loudly and with more bravado than she felt. "Are you afraid somebody will recognize you here in Nashville?"

He grunted and sat down on the back row next to the wall where he could watch everybody who came and went. When they heard her name called, he went to the desk with her and paid the entire fee up front, which came as a surprise to Myra.

She turned to him before going down the hall to change and held out her hand saying, "I'm sorry about all of this, Colson. I really loved you."

For a moment—a split second, really—it looked as though he, too, regretted the way things had turned out between them. She watched the shutter slide down, and instead of taking her hand he said, "Ungrateful whore! Watch your back," turned on his heel and left the building, seething.

Waiting just outside were Officer Max Eastonberry, some of Nashville's finest, and a lone woman who looked vaguely familiar. She approached him, and when she spoke, she saw with intense gratification the surprise on his face.

"Colson? Did you get another poor woman in trouble?" said his wife with deep sarcasm.

"Madge?" he stopped and stared at her, saying, "How on earth did you find me?" shock in his voice. Then he saw Eastonberry approaching from the side, and it finally dawned on him the gig was up.

Those big blue eyes turned wild when he panicked, both fists clenched tight.

"You are under arrest for multiple charges of theft, Colson Davis. Stand with your back to me," said Eastonberry as he began to cuff the man. Davis, however, had leaving on his mind and spun around, catching the officer by surprise.

"I don't think so," said Davis as he punched Eastonberry in the belly and ran for the black Mercury, losing his hat in the process. The great mane of silvery, black hair flew in the wind as he jumped into the car and gunned the engine. Barely missing Eastonberry and the Nashville officers, he backed out of the parking lot, tires squealing. Approaching the intersection at a high rate of speed, he ran squarely into a mint green Ford Galaxy made of solid steel that blocked his escape, expertly piloted by Miss Annie Pearl Dalrymple.

The Mercury spun out of control on impact, leaving skid marks all over the drive. The big black car finally flipped on the curb, landing upside down, its wheels spinning all the way to nowhere. Colson Davis lay face down in the open ditch underneath the car.

Ignoring him, Eastonberry ran to the familiar green Ford, which lay on its side. He and his fellow officers were able to tip it upright; he opened the driver's door, heavily dented from the crash, to find two women: Annie Pearl Dalrymple and Luanne Bugtussle. Both were laughing hysterically.

"That was a fine bit of driving, Annie Pearl Dalrymple, you foolish woman!" he cried. "And Mrs. Bugtussle—what on earth are you doing here? You two should not have put your lives at risk like that." Glancing back at Davis, who was apparently unconscious, he added with a grin, "But I do believe you stopped Preacher Colson Davis in his tracks."

The first responders set about stabilizing the situation, extracting the women, and getting them to the hospital. They had to move Colson Davis' car before a stretcher could take him to a waiting ambulance.

Eastonberry shook hands with his fellow officers and asked them to escort Madge Davis to his office in Loganton for questioning while he went in to wait for Myra Ledbetter's release from her procedure. She was groggy, pale, and shaken when she came out, but brightened considerably when he told her what had happened while she was in surgery.

Silent on the way back home, she lay in the backseat of his car, huddled under a blanket listening. When she finally spoke, it tore at him to hear the tears in her voice, "My baby was already dead, Officer Eastonberry. I knew before I came here. In a way, I'm glad. I wouldn't have wanted to bring a child into the world in a situation like that anyway. I couldn't possibly have aborted a live fetus: I never had a baby of my own."

They drove in silence the rest of the way, and when he took her home he wished Annie Pearl was there with them, but Ms. Dalrymple and Ms. Bugtussle were already busy meeting the press who were eager for the dirt on Colson Davis.

Miraculously, they were able to downplay Myra's part in the affair, thanks in good part to the acerbic verbiage from his wife, Madge Davis. When she finished describing his desertion of her and the children, and the embezzlement from the church, Myra was way down on their list of potential interviewees. She stayed at Annie Pearl's for a few days, trying to heal from the impossible hurt, both to her heart and to her body.

On the day she was to leave—she had decided to return to the mountains in Weaverville, North Carolina, to live with her parents— Luanne Bugtussle arrived with a gift, surprising both Myra and her hostess.

"No, no, you stay right where you are, young woman," said Luanne. Myra smiled wryly at the phrase *young woman*. She'd never felt as old in her life as she did at that moment. "The members of Cloud Level Primitive Baptist Church have a lot of apologizing to do to you Myra Ledbetter. One and all," she said, glancing swiftly at Annie Pearl, "we judged you without looking beyond what we could see right in front of our faces. Can you forgive us?"

Again, Myra started to speak, but Luanne held up her hand. "No, let me finish. The board asked me to present you with this check for helping us catch that awful man, and our apology for the way we treated you, dear. Take it with our blessing."

It was a check for $1,000 payable to Myra Ledbetter.

Just before Myra left, she served as Annie Pearl's maid-of-honor when she married Max Eastonberry at the Cloud Level Primitive Baptist Church. Packed to the rafters with well-wishers, the congregation stared in awe as Luanne Bugtussle walked the bride-to-be down the aisle and presented her to Max.

When they drove away in the mint green Ford, carefully restored by Leroy Grainger, Joe, and Buck, a little black bow flew out of the car and into the wind, caught by none other than Luanne Bugtussle.

On the Track

Found,
in a bed of red and white Impatiens
at an abandoned railroad track,
a dead cat.

Leaning against the rail of a defunct Southern Pacific
Pullman,
bones encased in a sack of skin,
dusty patches of off-white fur,
paw still up—
caught in the sacred ritual of bathing—
face obliterated by one shot to the head.

The train, a forgotten cylinder of rusted metal,
now a reminder of another lifetime:
high-back seats—
cracked, red leather still bearing
impressions from past lives…
linen pillows collapsed,
white goose feathers spilled out to fly no more.

Suspicious Remains

An Annie Pearl Dalrymple Mystery II

Millie Nolan watched Annie Pearl Dalrymple back out of her driveway and turn in the general direction of downtown Loganton, Tennessee. When the venerable Ford Galaxy was out of sight, she made her approach, staying close to a dense hedge of purple hydrangeas. She lucked out with a side window, barely open an inch, and raised it just enough to squeeze through. As soon as she raised it, Buster, the resident Yorkshire terrier. raised a ruckus, barking nonstop.

"Shut up, you stupid little mutt," she growled at the dog. The five-pound Yorkie bravely ignored the command, barking as if his life depended on it, his whole body lifting off the floor with the effort to sound.

In desperation, Millie snatched the baby blue chenille spread off the bed and threw it over the tiny dog. Buster, stymied, continued to bark—albeit muffled, confined at last. With great stealth, the woman crept through the house, taking two freshly baked, oatmeal, chocolate chip cookies from the kitchen table for sustenance. Surely, when she heard what Millie had to say, the old lady wouldn't miss a cookie or two.

Millie was surprised at how clean and fresh smelling the small house was. After prowling throughout, she reached the living room and chose a rocker by the window to await Ms. Dalrymple's return.

She'd been trying to reach Annie Pearl on the sly for days, but the woman was simply not available; she either had appointments or was just plain gone. Millie had good reason to want to avoid Ms. Dalrymple's companion, Officer Eastonberry. He was the town's sole enforcer of the law, and they had met on a previous occasion.

She'd been watching Annie Pearl's house for a number of days and noticed Officer Eastonberry stopped by every afternoon around 5 p.m. He often stayed for several hours and left with Annie Pearl standing in the door. My, my, she thought, nibbling a cookie, I do wonder what the fine, pious townsfolk would think if they knew their precious Annie Pearl was cavorting with the town's only police officer of an afternoon. What she didn't know was that the officer and Ms. Dalrymple had been married for a couple of months. Nor did she know that he took an afternoon break before heading back out to corral the town's few drunks into the jail for the night.

Lulled by the cookies and soft sunshine filtering in through the window, Millie was almost asleep when Buster fired off again. "Buster?" said Annie Pearl, in her southern country voice. "Where are you, Sugar? I've got a treat for you."

When the Yorkie failed to appear but continued to bark and whine, Annie Pearl mounted a search of the tiny house, finding him tangled in the bedspread. By this time, Millie was wide-awake; when the little terror came flying into the living room, teeth bared, she regretted not bribing him. He had her cornered in no time, feet off the ground. The final blow was when he lifted one leg.

"No, you damned dog," she yelled, "don't you dare—" But it was too late—Buster baptized her leg, purse, notebook, and recorder.

"Who might you be?" asked Annie Pearl in a cold voice, "And how dare you use foul language in my house?" She raised the kitchen broom. "What do you mean by trapping my Buster under the spread like that? He could have suffocated under there." Millie cringed as Annie Pearl moved closer. "*Again,* who are you and what are you doing in my house?"

Stammering in response, Millie was at a loss for words as the mild-mannered Annie Pearl Dalrymple, now a red-faced demon, brandished the broom at her. Keeping her feet off the floor, she tried to answer. "Please, Ms. Dalrymple, I meant no harm; believe me," she pleaded. "I've been trying to reach you, and you've not returned my calls, nor have you answered the door when I knocked. It seemed to me the best way to see you was to get into the house and wait."

The woman cowering in front of her looked perfectly ludicrous with her feet on the edge of the rocking chair. Annie Pearl hid a smile and responded with, "Well, I have been busy of late. Now you'd best get on with your business as I'm expecting Officer Eastonberry shortly, unless you wish to meet him, too. I would suggest you have a very good explanation handy. He's most protective of Buster and me."

Millie stared at the fierce little dog who vaguely reminded her of Annie Pearl. She feared any untoward movement would set him off again. "I really am sorry about the dog, and for breaking in like this, but I am desperate. I truly meant no harm," then added with a sheepish look on her long face, "surely, you can see that. He'll be okay, won't he?"

With a stern and forbidding expression on her face, Annie Pearl picked Buster up, cradling him on her ample bosom. Still on alert, the dog watched Millie as his mistress searched him for damage. "He appears to be all right, no thanks to you, young lady," she said, still with more than a hint of frost in her voice.

Finally, Annie Pearl set the terrier down, got a washcloth and some vinegar, and helped the woman clean Buster's irritated commentary away.

By the time Officer Eastonberry arrived, the women were deep in conversation over rose-hip raspberry tea and oatmeal cookies. Still on guard, Buster would have none of it, so when the back door opened, Buster lamented again, loud and clear. Had he been a bird dog, his tiny black nose would have pointed at Millie Nolan, a paw would have been up and the tail straight out. As it was, there was no doubt of Buster's displeasure as the good officer lifted him in one hand and tucked the tiny dog under his arm.

When Eastonberry faced the women at the table, it was with a frown. He had seen Annie Pearl's visitor before—at his jail.

"Oh, Max, I'm so glad you've come home," said Annie Pearl, preening, "I believe you have met Ms. Nolan already?"

"I certainly have," he replied, a stern look on his face. "May I ask what you are doing here? You've managed to get into more trouble in two days than most folks do in a lifetime. Are you going to come clean, or shall I take you back to your jail suite for the evening?"

Millie looked apprehensive. She had only tried to access the jail's records—but Annie Pearl smiled and told Eastonberry to settle down and make himself some coffee. Still with the little dog under his arm, he did as she suggested and then sat down between the women to hear Millie's tale. It wasn't an especially pretty one.

"And there's a strong probability that she's still got their bodies on that property, possibly in those big white freezers.... Why would a widow living alone keep that many full-size freezers?"

"You said what?" the officer bellowed. "Who's got what on which property? Not in my town, they do not!"

Annie Pearl put her plump little hand on his and patted it. "Now, now, we must watch your blood pressure, Max. What we're hearin' is hearsay and this young lady—she's an investigator from Alabama; she came here to look into Luanne's past and has turned it into a story. There's nothing to prove that Luanne killed all those men and hid them on her property. Something would have come out long before now."

"Not necessarily, Ms. Dalrymple," Millie protested. "She's a pillar of the church and a social cornerstone around here. Who would dare suspect her?"

Just then two sets of eyes, three counting Buster's, stared at her, unblinking.

"Ms. Nolan, just what gives you the right to make such an accusation?" questioned the officer in his most stern, law enforcement voice. "These are serious charges to make against a member of our community. This kind of thing may happen in other places, but not in my town."

"That may be the way you want to think of your town, Officer Eastonberry," said Millie. "But my client believes her daddy was lured here, married, and murdered by Luanne Bugtussle, and rumor has it there is something very fishy about those freezers at her house."

Officer Eastonberry looked first at Annie Pearl and then at Millie Nolan before responding. "I repeat, how do you know she has those freezers in her house, and what gives you the right to accuse her in this way?"

Millie Nolan felt them watching her as she made her way back to the car. "Who does he think he is?" she muttered under her breath. "High and mighty police officer... more like Podunk policeman who never left home. His mother probably still washes his clothes and irons his undershorts. No wonder that woman got away with murder right under his nose."

***

Annie Pearl and Max discussed Millie's assertions. "I know it sounds impossible," said Annie Pearl. "But I do recall the care she takes with those freezers—there *are* four of them, and I believe she had seven husbands at last count. I never understood it, the shriveled up old biddy…." She stopped and looked up at him, batting sparse eyelashes. "Oh, I'm so sorry. Forgive me."

"That's okay, Annie Pearl," he said. "I know she has been the bane of your existence forever; still there is something odd and strangely familiar with all of this."

Annie Pearl and Officer Eastonberry spoke of the situation at length. They finally decided Annie Pearl should pay Luanne a visit to let her know what Millie Nolan was saying about her. Max promised to be nearby in case of trouble.

***

When Millie reached her car in the next block, the stench of cat pee assaulted her senses. Dark spots of urine stained all four of her roommate's brand new tires. "Well, I'll be damned…." She snorted and then stopped in her tracks as Annie Pearl drove by in her mint green Ford at a dignified, sedate speed. At least Millie assumed she was driving the car—the woman was so short you couldn't even see the top of her head.

Ignoring the pervasive odor that assailed her senses, Millie climbed into the Datsun and pulled onto the road with the intention of following the Ford at a discreet distance. When Annie Pearl turned into a driveway just ahead, Millie parked under the shade of an old oak tree to wait. As she watched, a shadow darkened her door. Looking up, she found herself confronting the steadfast Officer Eastonberry.

Steel gray eyes stared into hot green ones, neither giving way to the other, until he spoke. "Are you aware you are driving in my town with an expired tag, Ms. Nolan?" He allowed a bit more drawl than necessary when he spoke her name and grinned at her obvious irritation.

"Why no, I didn't. You see, this really isn't exactly my car, Officer. I'm just borrowing it," she replied, pure loathing coating every word she uttered.

For once, she was telling the truth, except she left out the part about not telling her roommate she was going to borrow the car.

Officer Eastonberry stared at her for a moment then said, "Is your name really Millie Nolan, ma'am?" When she nodded, he added, "I'm going to give you the benefit of a doubt, just for today, but I would suggest you tell whoever owns this car they'd better get that tag renewed. Considering everything you've been into since you got here, I'm sure you won't mind if I write you a ticket." With that, he leaned against the car and leisurely wrote out a ticket in longhand as she watched Annie Pearl go up the steps to Luanne Bugtussle's front porch. Fuming, she raged inwardly, but she knew Eastonberry had her on this one, and she couldn't risk raising his ire any further. She tried unsuccessfully to peer around the big man, but could not see past his starched uniform.

***

Puffing as she went, Annie Pearl struggled up to the front porch between banks of deep red begonias dripping like blood onto gleaming white concrete steps. Exertion, anxiety, and anticipation reddened her fair skin. In all the years the two women had sparred for first place in their community, this was only the second time she had come up those steps. The first was when she welcomed Luanne and her husband Henry to town. It was then she first recognized a rival in the newcomer, but feeling secure in her place as the hometown girl, she had paid little attention to it. That was her first mistake. The second was caring what the thin, sprightly woman thought about her, but she did. Oh, yes, she surely did care.

Back at the curb, Millie peered anxiously around the tall officer, but he stayed right where he was. Then he wrinkled his nose and sneezed, saying, "By the way, I believe a cat has sprayed your tires, ma'am. You might want to invest in a couple of cans of tomato juice… just like you would for a skunk… that might help." Grinning, he walked off as Annie Pearl disappeared inside Luanne's front door.

When Annie Pearl pulled the shiny brass doorknocker, she was almost surprised when Luanne came to the door. For her part, Luanne was shocked to see Annie Pearl standing under the ferns on her front porch. After a temporary alliance to cast their errant preacher out of his pulpit and bring his sins to light, they had resumed their customary distance; Luanne saw no reason to alter that course. Annie Pearl, however, looked flushed and unnatural to her shrewd eye.

"And what is it that brings you to my door, Annie Pearl? Do you need something?" There was no warmth in the cool, polite greeting and no invitation to enter the house.

"If you will let me inside, I will try to tell you," said Annie Pearl, sliding past a visibly irritated Luanne. She went straight to the front room and settled her girth onto one of Luanne's most prized possessions, a fragile Queen Ann side chair.

Forgoing the usual polite preamble, Annie Pearl plunged into the reason for her visit while Luanne, sitting primly on the edge of her chair, paled. At the end of Annie Pearl's report, Luanne leaned back and said nothing for some time. When finally she sat upright and spoke, she told a tale Annie Pearl wished devoutly for the rest of her life she'd never heard.

Finally, the lurid tale released from her keeping, Luanne leaned back, her eyes closed, one thin white hand etched in spidery blue veins cupped over her mouth.

Stunned by the revelation, Annie Pearl waited, but Luanne remained as she was—cool and still. "Mr. Eastonberry, are you there?" she called out in a panicked, hoarse voice.

Within two minutes, the tall lawman was standing beside her. He checked Luanne's pulse and said, "It's either a cold faint or a stroke." He called the emergency squad and set to work on resuscitating Luanne to no avail. Luanne Bugtussle lay where she was, the neatly pressed, light blue, cotton shirtwaist barely awry. Finally, he stood back and put a protective arm around Annie Pearl.

"Oh, my goodness; I had no idea this would happen," Annie Pearl said, leaning against him. She looked up just in time to see Millie Nolan creeping off the porch, camera in hand.

"It's that awful woman—Millie Nolan!" she said, pointing at Millie's retreating figure. "The Lord help us if she heard what Luanne confessed in this room today. Such a tale I never thought to hear in all my days."

"I doubt she heard anything beyond our trying to resuscitate Ms. Bugtussle," he said. "Can you tell me what you said to her?" asked the officer, duty overcoming his desire to protect Annie Pearl.

"I simply told her what that Millie Nolan told us a while ago. You should have seen Luanne's face when I got to the part about all those husbands in the freezers...."

"Husbands in the freezers?" he repeated after her. "You're telling me there really are bodies in those freezers?" he asked, horror showing in his face.

"Luanne killed poor Henry, Mr. Eastonberry. She thought he was about to run out on her, so she stopped him. However, he wasn't the first; she killed all of her husbands: Henry, James, George, Francis, Robert, and her own father—he was the first... that was in South Alabama where she was born... that one, I cannot fault her for killing."

Abruptly, Annie Pearl stopped, mid-sentence. Her skin took on a strangely green tint as she turned to the door. "Please don't ask me any more for now. I'm going to be sick." With that, she made her way to the front porch and vomited all over the lovely, red flowers while the officer gently held her head and patted her heaving back.

Shortly thereafter, the first responders arrived, followed by an ambulance. When they got no response, they rolled the ill-fated Luanne Bugtussle out of her spotless front room, down the gleaming, white steps, and into the waiting ambulance, leaving without sounding the siren. The good officer secured the house and escorted Annie Pearl home. A quick call to the courthouse got Judge Parker to issue a search warrant, after which he returned to the scene of the crime. Correction: crimes. What he found sickened him to the core, but he was an officer of the law and was above allowing fragile human emotions to control his actions, or so he thought.

In Luanne's impeccably clean, white kitchen freezer, he found Henry, his body parts neatly wrapped in white butcher paper, neatly labeled with his name and the date. On the back porch, he found three more freezers, and in them were James, George, Francis, and Robert. It was then that his body betrayed him, and he puked into the lilies that grew in abundance just outside the back door—poisonous belladonna they were, growing in glorious profusion in the backyard.

The next morning, Loganton's papers were full of the story and by nightfall, every small town broadsheet in the south reported on the venomous Luanne Bugtussle, now a living corpse, lying in the county hospital in Loganton. Forensic investigator Millie Nolan became an overnight sensation, as she was the one who broke the news. Giddy with excitement, she exploited every minute of airtime and print space she could get, telling the story about Luanne's knife collection and the fabulous garden filled with the belladonna lilies that she used to kill her husbands. She dared not return to Officer Eastonberry's town, though, for its citizens had drawn together in an effort to protect Annie Pearl. Had she gone back, they would surely have run her out of town. Worse, they might have punctured her tires and made her stay....

Even after the exhumation of her father's remains, Luanne's story simmered on for nearly a year. Experts of every ilk had something to say, and they said it often, and on camera. Annie Pearl, devastated by Luanne's story and the publicity it generated, refused to speak to reporters of any kind and stayed behind the scenes as much as possible.

It turned out that Luanne grew up on the outskirts of Birmingham, Alabama. Her mother died when she was a youngster, leaving the girl to the mercies of her stern father. When she caught the eye of a young man at church, he came courting, much to her father's disapproval. The widower turned him away and locked his daughter in her room, but the youngsters finally found a way of escape and ran away together. When her father found them, he killed the boy, took his daughter home, and raped her, shredding what little dignity she had left. He told her that if she wanted to sleep with a man, fine, but to remember always that it would be him that she bedded.

Life became a living hell for the young girl with, seemingly, no way out. After numerous miscarriages—all the infants her father threw in the hog pen—she finally killed him with his own butcher knife as he slept in her bed. That was her first experience in butchery, but the hogs had no worries with her inexperienced cutting and ravenously ate the evidence. Shortly thereafter, she dug up the money the widower had buried in the sawdust pile and made her way into Birmingham. It was there she met her first husband. When he displeased her, by that time, she knew what to do.

***

One night, when the storm surrounding the murders had settled into a mild roar, Annie Pearl Dalrymple Eastonberry snuggled up to her husband, almost purring. Then she said in a low, soft voice, "Mr.

Eastonberry, now that I know how Luanne killed her husbands, I'd advise you to behave, if you know what is good for you."

When she chuckled, kissing him playfully, it drove everything from his mind but that warm, soft body next to his. Annie Pearl had surprised him—she was a sensual creature whose every instinct knew how to arouse him.

The next morning, however, what she had said came back to haunt him. In truth, that comment bothered him for the rest of their long and happy lives. To make very sure she had no reason for vengeance, he was always good and kind to her. However, just in case, and by way of insurance, he kept their knives dull and then destroyed every belladonna lily in the region.

The Last Cypress Tree

Walking deep in the forest one day, I came upon a tree
rooted securely deep in earth's mire,
trunk soaring high—
I felt its essence to be strong.

"Touch me," said the Tree,
and I did.

Warmth surged through me as fire from a lover's hand,
I moved away, frightened by feelings aroused within.

"Touch me," said the Tree,
and I did.

Reaching out my hand, I knew I wanted it to be more—
I leaned into its massive trunk, and there knew completion.
Joined to life's source,
rooted in mother earth,
skin cooled in its gentle shade,
I reached out through the tree's branches.

Now at peace, at one with my world,
life's passions and conflicts settled,
joined with Great Mother through her creation.

The Tree of Life

Blue Lightning

My dad, Ferd Gerrell, was born in North Florida in a tiny town named Woodville. Arriving not long after Florida achieved statehood in the early 1800s, the family of Florida Crackers had farmed and timbered the land for almost ninety years by the time this story occurred.

The family farm was near the St. Marks River, which joins the Wakulla to drain into the Gulf of Mexico. My dad and his brother left school to help their mother and three sisters with the farm when his father died.

Florida's sandy soil is fragile, and while fertile in the beginning, farmland wrangled from swampy jungles soon becomes unproductive. It took all their mother could do to keep the family sheltered, fed, and clothed.

One morning over a breakfast of fatback, grits and biscuits, she told them a storm was coming—a hurricane. All the signs pointed to it, and she figured they might be directly in its path. All five children had assignments: bring the cattle in, tie everything down, and hope for the best. One of Ferd's regular jobs was rounding up the cattle for counting and branding. When he heard what he had to do that day, however, fear rode out with him. He didn't much like riding, but that was the only way he had of getting those long-horned bovines out of the woods and into the corral. He saddled the little Florida Cracker pony named Gracie, and then called the cur dog, Joe, and set out on his journey.

All went well for most of that hot summer day. Knowing where their branded herd grazed, his little team ferreted the livestock from the sand-hills, savannahs, and bogs, but when it came to the St. Marks River, special methods were required. It seemed to him the sky had never been so blue, the grass so green, nor the air so pure, but as the sun began to drop, the wind picked up.

The cattle liked to graze on the bottom grass in the shallows of the river on hot summer days. Joe's specialty just happened to be convincing the semi-wild cattle to come up out of the river bottom where they loved to cool their heels, grazing on the eelgrass. The dog slid down the bank into the shallows and began to nip their heels. Soon, those stubborn bovines gave up their delectable, green ribbons to stomp their way out to dry land, but they were far from happy about it.

The wind's fury was fast picking up, and the boy knew they'd not make it home before sundown. Still, his whip at the ready, he urged them on. The cattle were nervous, Gracie was nervous, and so was he; Joe was just doing his job. When they reached the Shepherd Spring, thunder began to roil in the distance, and suddenly, the wind's speed ratcheted up to gale force, pushing the herd forward. One steer, long a troublemaker, tried to cut from the herd. No sooner had it made a bid for freedom than Ferd's whip cracked over the tip of its widespread horns. With no warning, a single finger of cerulean danced through the sky to touch the whip's tip and then snaked up the whip's straight line to envelop both horse and rider. Shimmering azure light leapt from one rack of long horns to the next, ghostly, glowing fingers immersing the entire herd in shades of blue.

When a golden streak of lighting struck a deadhead cypress tree on the trail nearby, it exploded in a fiery detonation of sparks and splinters. The cattle split, Joe headed home and the *cracker pony* took off, too, blinded with fear. Sitting low, the boy gripped her mane in his teeth and her sides with his legs. They rode for what seemed to be miles until that valiant pony's hoof caught in a root, sending the boy head over heels into the air.

"Ferd? Wake up." As from a distance, he heard an eerie voice calling him by name, but he couldn't respond. "Boy, I said wake up, and I mean for you to do it now!" Again, he tried to come out of shock's fierce grip. Rain pelted his face as the gods of wind and storm rode over him. "Son, you have to get up," came the shrill voice yet again. "There ain't room in here for two. Besides that, you're too young. GET UP!"

Finally, the voice of the sunken grave's original occupant got through to him, and the boy began to stir.

Feeling around for something to grab hold of, he picked up an object that felt cool and firm to the touch. Lightning struck again, lighting up the darkness, and that is when he realized what was in his hand; it was a bone, a human bone. Screaming, he tried to stand, but the ground was slippery under his feet. Sliding down into a bed of bones, he cried out, "Joe, come help me!"

Joe, that wise old dog, lay dry as a bone under the house, but when he heard the boy's call, he raised his head and let out a bay heard over the cry of the storm. When it finally stopped, two long ears flapped over the side of the grave as Joe tried to reach his master.

"No, Joe—not me. Find Gracie, find Gracie." Now, Ferd always said Joe was smarter than your average human being, and this day's events proved it true. The dog found the horse, shaken, but unhurt, and herded her to the grave, finding the boy surrounded by rising water and swirling bones of white.

"Bring her to me, Joe," and that is exactly what that old dog did. Nipping at the little pony's heels, he brought her to the grave's edge. When the reins dropped into the depression, the boy grabbed them and pulled himself out.

He climbed on Gracie's back, ready for the ride home when he saw his bedraggled dog looking up at him, rain pouring down his long ears and dripping from his short tail. "Hey, Joe, you want a ride home?" Joe had never been on a horse, to be sure, but he rode home in front of the boy that night.

***

The boy's mother was standing in the door, waiting with a lantern, having heard Joe baying over the storm. "Take the horse to the barn, son, and come back quick as you can." With bent heads, boy and horse made their way to the stable, but Ferd stopped suddenly. In the corral was the herd, safe.

He looked down at his dog and said, "Joe, you want to come inside the house tonight?"

Joe, a farm dog to the core, had never been in the house, but he went inside that night. He ate from Ferd's plate, and when it was time to go to bed, old Joe slept at the foot of the boy's bed. The storm, raging outside, rattled the shutters, but it bothered him not at all. He was safe, he had done his job well, his belly was full, and he slept next to his best friend.

***

The next morning dawned clean and clear. The storm had brushed past the little cabin in the woods, leaving downed trees and ruined fields in its wake, but all was safe with the little family. When Ferd woke to a warm dog nestled at his feet, he sat up, stared at him, and then said, "I'm going to give you a new name, boy. Blue Lightning!" And that is how a hound named Joe saved the day and got his new name.

Moment In Time

Rain came down in fierce torrents,
gusting wind blasted slick, wet windows.
Storm-crazed gods roiled above,
casting lightning bolts
through angry black clouds.

Birds found sanctuary in dim tree cavities,
but safe inside,
we watched nature wear herself out,
raging against trunk, limb, leaf, and wing.

A young boy watched nearby,
brown eyes staring in wonder at nature's fury.

Hair tussled and damp,
tiny tear-shaped dewdrops
clung to tender ear lobes.
Glistening crystal clear,
like diamonds they hung—
innocence, and lack of awareness
part of the moment.

Note: At the Tallahassee Museum of Natural History

Gator Giggin' in Blackwater Swamp

It was Sunday, and the sun was barely up when two boys rode into the dense fog in a rickety wagon, pulled by one stubborn old mule named Suki. They spoke in excited whispers as they watched for gator slides on the banks of the creek they followed into Blackwater Swamp.

Slowly the mule made its way through the thick undergrowth of palmetto, bog buttons, and jack-in-the-pulpit as the sun rose higher into the hot summer sky, but the boys didn't see any of it. The wagon's wheels stuck in the thick muck, and once, their boat nearly bounced out of the back. It didn't stop them for a minute; they had a job to do—they were going gator giggin'.

The fog was breaking up by the time they reached the creek and it was getting hot. Their thin homespun shirts were soaked with sweat, their hair plastered to their heads, and they were thirsty, but nothing quelled their excitement. I take that back—when mosquitoes descended like a cloud around the wagon, threatening to devour them and Suki, they very nearly panicked. Wilmer lit a pilfered pipe and started blowing smoke all around them. That helped, but the poor mule just had to tolerate the winged plague that stuck to her like glue.

***

Suki kept on, as though each step might be her last, occasionally trying to look back at them and rolling her eyes in protest. The boys ignored her, regaling themselves with memories of past gator hunts, speaking in hushed tones of a legendary ghost gator said to haunt the swamps at night.

Suddenly, Ferd cried out, "Look Wilmer," pointing to the shallow pool below. "That's it—the old gator's wallerin' hole, and look how

122

wide that tail slide is—I've never seen a gator that could make a swath that big. That's got to be the one we're lookin' for!"

Sure enough, directly off the track, Wilmer saw the wide, beaten path made by the tail of a huge alligator. It led straight down to the shallow pond and disappeared in the dark water below. There were other slides nearby, but this one had to be it. They had been searching for the big gator's den for some time, and surely now they had found it… the home of the great-great-grandfather of all gators.

Wilmer nodded, pulled on the reins, and snuffed the smoking pipe out. He jerked the felt hat down low over his ears to escape the buzzing mosquitoes and the no-see-ums that attacked him. He grabbed the long stick with the metal hook and the rope, climbed out, and then tied the reins to a sapling. Ferd took the carbide lanterns—this was before flashlights—carbide illuminates when it is wet. Suki, the mule, glad of a rest, dropped her head to nibble wiregrass.

Together, the boys pulled the little boat out of the back of the wagon and let it slide gently down the bank. With the carbide lanterns strapped securely on their heads, they crawled into the marshy shallows and waited on their bellies in the bottom of the boat, hoping for their quarry to make an appearance.

They waited a long time, so long they nearly fell asleep. There was no movement in the water, just mosquitoes and dragonflies buzzing overhead.

Finally, a small, juvenile alligator swam near the boat and Wilmer grabbed it and held it up, letting it cry in distress… hoping the old gator might respond to its cry. There was no response from the dark hole which was the entrance to the gator's den.

"Ferd, this ain't gonna work," said the older brother, dropping the feisty little alligator back into the water. "We gotta get real serious. Let's wet our lanterns to get them lit, so we can see down there."

Ferd's eyebrows climbed high when Wilmer got the pole with the metal hook out and climbed into the water. He half-waded and half-swam to the entrance to the gator's den and started poking around in the cavity. He could see something in there, possibly a tail, but he couldn't be sure, so he reached in as far as he could. This time, he hit pay dirt, but the payout was more than he bargained for.

Suddenly, a monstrously huge gator came backing out of the den tail first, making the loud, gasping grunt that said the old gator was angry, and somebody would pay for it. More and more gator emerged from the deep hole as the boy drew back in horror. Hissing, the gigantic, toothy mouth snapped wide open in fury as its owner looked for the culprit who dared to disturb the gator's peace and tranquility.

Ferd fell out of the boat and into deeper water, floundering in surprise. Panicked and unable to feel the pond's bottom, Wilmer desperately stabbed at the big reptile, trying to find the kill spot between the eyes, but he knew it was a losing battle.

Whether it was by accident or a genuine miracle, the hook made purchase and struck the mark. The huge alligator arched its back and flung Wilmer against the bank where he lay stunned, his head barely above the water. Before it finally rolled over and went belly up, the old gator churned the water until it was a dark, brown mass of bloody mud. Out of breath and still frightened, both of the boys sat in the reddening, shallow water, trying to catch their breath, until Ferd grinned at his older brother.

"We did it, Brother; we got the big one," he said, laughing and shaking his red head. His brother Wilmer, who was still scowling over the risk they had taken and the knowledge that he could have gotten them both killed, looked up, and then he grinned too. "I believe we did, little Brother. Now, we have to face our mama and tell *her* what we just did. I'd rather meet another wild gator than tangle with her."

The deed was done, however, and it was too late to change anything. Together they tied the gator's snout with the rope, looped it under its front armpits, and then dragged the long, heavy body up its own grass slide to the wagon, using one of Ferd's inventions—a winding winch—and tied it off to the seat. This left the thick tail to drag behind on the trip back home. They had the gator secured, but wise old Suki, a concerned look on her grizzled face, refused to budge.

Nothing they did persuaded that mule to move until Wilmer prodded it in the rear with the metal hook. The mule jerked its head up, rolled its eyes back so far you could see the whites, and charged ahead. Wilmer had to jump onto Suki, crawl over her back, and leap into the wagon, she was moving so fast.

The sun was setting when they finally saw the lights of home in the distance. They had missed school that day and supper that night. Both boys were starving, thinking of little but food and a warm bed. Then all hell broke loose. The wagon rattled, and Suki stopped mid-stride. The boys looked at one another in surprise; the wagon shook hard again.

"He ain't dead, Brother!" cried Ferd in fright. "That gator's done come back to life! It's magic; that's what it is."

Quickly, Wilmer grabbed the hook pole and told his brother to jump out and grab the gator's tail. Running to the back of the wagon, Ferd caught the vicious tail as the old gator fought valiantly for its life. The rope held the gator's head and front legs in place, but everything else moved. The scaly tail flung the boy against the sides of the wagon, the sides popping and cracking every time he slammed into them.

"Do something quick, Wilmer," he cried, holding on for a life that suddenly felt extremely precious to him. "I can't do this much longer!"

The older boy stood, bracing himself in an iron grip, with a calmness he did not feel on the wagon seat. Waiting for the right moment to strike, he took aim at the alligator's head. He had to hit smack between the eyes or at the side of the eyes to kill the reptile. He was desperately afraid he'd lose his grip, but the strike proved true. The metal hook pierced the gator clean between the eyes and it moved no more.

Wise old Suki rolled her eyes so far back they stuck that way. The old mule refused to move an inch, not for quite some time. This time around, nothing, and no one could make that mule move an inch until she was very sure that gator was never going to move again.

It was just before sunup the next morning when Suki finally reckoned the gator was dead and took them home. Covered in blood, bruised and battered, both dreaded facing their mother. They foolishly thought she'd still be abed; that is, until they heard her calling them. As Suki approached the gate, their mother ran toward them—lantern in hand, fear in her voice. Their sisters followed close behind, stopping when they saw what was in the back of the wagon, the long tail dragging in the sand.

"Where have you boys been? What have you done? Are you hurt?" Words filled with anguish, anger, and fear tumbled from their mother's mouth and those of their sisters, but the two boys were as silent as the mule. They just sat there, mute, and unable to respond.

They missed school that day, as the gator's meat and hide were too valuable to lose to decay and spoilage, but they were also on restrictions—the worst they had ever known. No adventures, no leaving home at night, church every Sunday—no skipping; they had to do all their homework, milk the cow, groom Gracie, feed the chickens, plow the fields, and sweep the yard to keep the snakes out... but secretly, they knew their mother appreciated what they had done. Times were hard, and they needed the money.

They took the hide to the dock at Newport on the St. Marks River and sold the meat to folks with a taste for gator, trading for produce in exchange for the meat. They got big money for the hide of that fifteen-foot alligator—a nickel with an American Indian's head on it.

What they didn't see was the soft, eerie light that followed them all the way home that night. They had missed the big one—the true swamp mystery—the legendary ghost gator, but it had not missed them.

We'll save that story for another day.

Raptor's Lament

Eagle, osprey, hawk—
aerial masters all,
once built places of refuge
in ancient trees.

Their progeny, raised in
ancestral watchtowers,
flew wild—
untethered, free.

Enter man,
bringing with him
a specter of progress,
shadows cast in blueprint over
nature's bounty.

Bulldozers rampaged through old forests
leaving in their wake
strange rivers of black asphalt,
houses with cold square eyes…
and,
oh, yes—
plywood platforms set upon slick, straight poles…
new aeries… a kind gesture… how thoughtful!

PART III

RUMINATION

Lessons for the Errant

Pain has a way of
catching one off-guard,
impressing itself into the psyche,
throbbing like a toothache
that won't go away.

Discomfort comes in all flavors
with lessons to be learned
That might have been easier
to bear
had we listened sooner.

Agony socks it to us
in ways we will remember—
thwacking, smacking, walloping wounds
all in an effort
perhaps…
to aid in
avoiding life's most onerous chore—
repetition.

Almost Left Behind

My grandmother, Lockey Crystelle Austin, was a tall, angular woman in a day when desirable women were soft and rounded. Far too intelligent and independent to be properly submissive, her family had no idea what to do with her: an unmarried woman with no prospects in a tiny, inbred town. Fortunately, she had an aunt who ran a boarding house in a temporary timber town that needed a baker. It was there that she perfected the fine art of biscuit making, baking from sunup to sundown.

While she was making those fine biscuits the size of a man's palm, she found a husband, a cedar-shake shingle maker by profession. A robust, darkly handsome man with hazel eyes and a warm smile, Albert Franklin Connell was in need of a wife. After their marriage, they lived in one of the tiny, mobile shacks provided by the railroad for the timber men and their families.

A gifted craftswoman, Grandmother moved from biscuit maker to tailor after the birth of her first child. When they moved to town, she was soon ensconced in a fine women's wear shop as the tailor. Of the Holiness faith, she wore her prematurely snow-white hair in an elegant bun on the back of her head without a speck of makeup on her face. Yet, she wore the store's fine suits with the élan of a fashion model. As she grew older, I recall many a rainy afternoon, playing dress-up in her bedroom, suit skirts dragging the floor, sleeves past my knees, a dainty hat perched on my head.

When Jackie Kennedy introduced the pillbox hat, my grandmother fell head over heels for the look and bought one for every outfit she owned. She wore them pushed straight down on her high forehead to compensate for the ever-present bun, making her look taller and more imposing than ever. I never saw her hair down—she always wore it in a bun.

She collected every strand of hair that fell from her head as she went from dark brown to gray, to white, conserving it in a cut-glass container. Grandmother's bun-bowl, as I called it, was a constant work in progress. Over the years, she created at least five full buns in distinct shades as her hair lightened. Eventually, when her hair became too thin, she simply attached one of her homemade buns, sometimes forgetting which shade matched her current hair color.

Growing up, I was practically her shadow. She taught me everything she could in an effort to make sure I attracted an appropriate husband, raised obedient children, and went to heaven when I died. She wanted to make certain that I graced the pearly gates when my time came. It grieved her soul when I grew wayward and started thinking for myself, but I had a model to follow there—my beautiful mother.

A lovely woman with flawless skin, flashing hazel eyes, dark, luxurious hair, and frustrated dreams, my mother fretted and chafed against Grandmother's strictures and demands based on her holiness beliefs. As a result, under Mother's tutelage and to my grandmother's dismay, I learned early on how to apply makeup. My mother tailored my clothes to be extremely revealing and sent me out into the world, unprepared for what that combination would do to me. My grandmother, however, knew exactly what could happen. The prospect of my descent into sin frightened her so badly that she literally hit the floor, supplicating for God's grace on my behalf on bended knees calloused from prayer. It seemed the Almighty ignored her pleas until the day, by purest accident, I found myself left behind.

Often, I went to my grandparent's house after school. It was a craftsman-style design that Granddaddy adapted to our Florida climate. Painted snow white with a big front porch and a back screened-in stoop overlooking his garden, it was spacious and airy in summer, and big and freezing cold in winter. I loved that house.

One day I arrived earlier than usual and skipping up the brick steps called out, "Grandmother, I'm here!" I got no answer. The screen door, with its heron decoration worked in metal, was unlatched, the front door stood open.

"Is anybody home?" I called again. Mother's car was in the driveway, Grandmother's was under the carport, and Granddaddy's big, blue Ford pickup was there, too, but all was silent. Growing concerned, I wandered around the house. The upright piano was open with sheet music on the stand, purses lay about untended, where were they? The kitchen spelled my undoing.

Grandmother's pride and joy, the red Formica and chrome dinette table and chairs was set for lunch, but something was wrong. Drawn back from the table were three chairs; food was still on the plates, ice melted in tall, green tea glasses, napkins lay strewn about in disarray. Grandmother's throw-cloth still hung on its rung by the stove—where were they?

Then it hit me, and I jumped to the most logical conclusion I could under the circumstances! Grandmother was right—all that stuff she tried to teach me was true; the Second Coming of the Lord was real. I would have to face the future alone. The Rapture of God's Chosen people had come and gone, and I had missed the cut. Even today, many, many years later, the very thought of that day is unsettling.

Wrapping my arms tightly around my body I collapsed in one of the chairs and began to cry, forgetting that unless Granddaddy had a complete change of mind at the last minute, he should still be around somewhere.

When I heard their voices and the screened door opened, I cried out in relief, running into their arms. As it turned out, one of the neighbors, Mrs. Diehl, took a bad fall and broke her hip. They heard her cry and all three—Grandmother, Granddaddy, and my mother—rushed to the rescue, hence their unplanned absence. I quickly came to myself but not in time to hide my predicament from my grandmother. She knew exactly what had happened to her wayward granddaughter, and I could tell from the sharp twinkle in her eye that she was going to use it for some time to come.

Butterfly in a Box

Butterfly in a glass box,
poised on a pedestal.

Butterfly in a box,
eyes that can see—blind.

Butterfly in a box,
wings that can fly—trapped.

Butterfly in a box,
wings hit glass—oh!

Butterfly in a box,
walls shatter—fear.

Butterfly, Butterfly
use your fear to fuel your flight.

Fly free Butterfly,
for you are me.

Third Grade Drama Queen

My third grade school picture shows a petite, dark-haired girl with a pug nose and a perky ponytail. A profile photo, it shows me looking into the distance with my eyes half-closed, almost dreaming. That it was prophetic never dawned on anyone until many, many years later.

I spent my formative years in something very close to heaven for an adventurous child. Born in the old Dale Mabry Army hospital in Tallahassee, Florida, in 1948, I grew up in a sage-green bungalow on the corner of Stadium Drive and Old St. Augustine Road with my family.

We were on the town side of the railroad tracks, which guaranteed excitement every day. My dad, a watchmaker and gemologist, was the official timekeeper of the Eastern Seaboard Coastal Railroad line, so we were interested in all the trains that passed by. Each one had a unique whistle, and soon, my brother and I knew them by heart. A number of hobos, ragged rail-riders who hopped from the trains nearby, made a beeline to our little house on the corner, because they knew my mother was a kind woman. She was always good for a glass of sweet iced tea and a sandwich, handed out the back screened door from our kitchen.

Just behind our house was a huge open ditch through which flowed downtown's runoff water. Much to our mom's distress, my brother and I spent many a happy hour there, chasing rain frogs and earthworms, sliding down its banks on slick, wet grass, but one day, she put a stop to it.

One year, after a mighty hurricane, the ditch overflowed and made our little house a small island. I can still see her, standing on the front porch, her hands held out over the rising water. "Oh, Lord," she prayed, "Please don't let that water get into my house!" Apparently, she had the Almighty's ear that day because those flood waters receded quickly

S. Kelley
The Day the Mirror Cried

after that. Later, waging a battle with City Hall, my mom made them cover that ditch, moving our little neighborhood up a notch while destroying our favorite playground.

Throughout the year, we heard Florida State University's band practicing in the stadium. We watched the players and cheerleaders perform their routines on the football field. We scrutinized college girls from our front porch as they teetered by on high heels, on the way to the games. We heard the screams of fans—the roars when they won, and the moans when they lost. The FSU circus practiced and performed under the big tents across West Pensacola Street, a short walk away. We saw and heard it all, and it was a fabulous and carefree time.

Life changed, however, when I entered first grade. School was okay, and I liked being with the other kids, but in class, I was slower than my classmates were. At first, they attributed this to my having been a wild child, but they couldn't ignore it forever. Arithmetic was my downfall; addition was troublesome, and by the time we got to subtraction, I was in deep trouble. While there was nothing wrong with my imagination, my list of woes grew daily, amplified by fear of failure. Learning to tie my shoes was impossible, and other things flew past me, too. Reading was my Waterloo—what was wrong with me?

One day, after practicing my multiplication tables hundreds of times to no avail, and then failing at reading, I found myself in an early version of a special needs class. Discussion of a learning disability never came up—I'm not sure such a thing had been heard of in those days. I can promise you, I learned a great deal from the experience. Being in that class was a revelation to be sure, and it was there, I first learned compassion. I soon became a fierce defender for those I felt were mistreated or misunderstood, a way of life that has endured to this day.

As I was at the FSU laboratory school, the tools were in place to try experimental learning, and I took to it eagerly. Once exposed to phonetics, I grasped the principle of sound related to shapes and to words. They spelled freedom to me, and I soon taught myself to read. Talk about liberating, words fail to describe what the opening of that window meant to me. The result was a lifetime love of learning and later, the discovery of an innate ability to improvise. Unfortunately, nothing ever helped with arithmetic. All I got from it was an intimate knowledge of shame and failure.

137

In third grade, I became a dreamer, creating stories as a way to deal with the situations that presented themselves to me. Our school was new and modern with banks of windows showing the ever-changing sky. I never tired of looking at the clouds, but it frequently got me in trouble. That year we had a unit on Helen Keller, and she soon became my hero. One day, I was in my usual spot in the back of the class, tracking a cluster of lush cumulus clouds, when Miss Carter, my teacher, said, "Saundra, look at the chalkboard, will you?" I must have looked dazed because she added, "Can't you see it, child?"

"No ma'am, not from here," I replied without a second thought to the lie.

"You come right up here, sweetheart," she said. "I didn't realize you were having trouble seeing from back there!"

I soon saw great value in the situation and before long was squinting at everything, drawing lots of attention. The day came when my teacher asked about my vision, so thinking of Helen Keller, without batting an eyelash, I told her I was going blind. From that moment on, life took on a pleasing twist with special treats, lunch brought to me, a guide in the halls—you name it. I loved every minute of it.

This went on for about a month and came to an abrupt end the day school let out for summer. Miss Carter assigned one of my best friends, a boy named George, to escort me to the picnic grounds outside near the FSU circus tents. He brought lunch to me while I held court, telling stories. I was regaling my friends when I heard a familiar voice—it was my mother. She had baked her prize-winning chocolate chip cupcakes as a surprise for my class. Miss Carter greeted her and pointed to my throne by the circus tents.

My mother's hair went white in her thirties, and her skin was very fair. That day, she wore a navy blue, polka-dot dress and her favorite white pumps. I squinted for real as she and Miss Carter talked, trying hard to read their lips. They frequently pointed to where I sat with my entourage. I saw my mother's face turn beet red; her white hair almost glowed in contrast. With that blue and white polka-dot dress, she looked like an artistic rendering of an angry, red, white, and blue American flag.

Without uttering a word, she stared straight at me, raised her arm, and pointed away from the picnic back toward our house. My head down, I rose, leaving my friends with mouths gaping, and then I walked straight to purgatory with perfect eyesight.

Punishment followed the crime, but my actions also got me some help. The special classes were good for me, allowing me the time I needed to figure things out at my own pace. I wonder to this day if I might never have learned to read or write without it, but what I was dealing with remained an unknown factor. I continued to feel shame and embarrassment, especially after returning to school in the fall to stories of my epic performance and tragic fall from grace. As with many folks who live with learning challenges, I learned to hide it at all costs, performing far below my true ability, turning inward. My life story consists largely of failure, humiliation, and lack of self-confidence and self-worth. A high intelligence quotient means nothing, if one cannot use it.

Because my school offered orchestra, chorus, theater, and art, I developed my expressive skills to a high degree. After graduating from high school, I made it through college, almost to graduation, but math and science again proved to be my downfall. I left school to avoid the shame of yet another failure.

Many years later, after marriage, two children, and divorce, I was better informed and less willing to accept failure. I had two girls to encourage, and I couldn't let them down. I won a scholarship from one of the earliest classes at FSU—it may have been 1948, and returned to school. This time, I knew I had to make it through to graduation. I no longer thought I was stupid, but I was also determined—two daughters watching every move I made. For a while, my girls and I were in school together, all three of us. I graduated with the eldest, but it was not without a mighty struggle.

I discovered a latent ability to solve problems without knowing how I did it. While it was by no means a perfect system, it got me through. I pulled it off somehow, but I was still mortally afraid of failure and exposure. I took a job with the good folks at Big Bend Hospice and embarked on a career using the persuasive skills I had learned so many years earlier. I loved it but felt there had to be more.

One serendipitous day, I met a woman named Robin who opened a magical door to me. She worked with an academy for folks with learning disabilities. As we spoke, I recognized much of what I had experienced in her descriptions of the work she did. I attended a seminar, and that's where my difficulties got names, not labels. dyslexia and dyscalculia. It was a relief to know what it was that circumvented so many of my attempts at learning, and it was there that I discovered empowerment. Soon, I began to seek out ways to stretch and learn. While I made some terrible mistakes, at least I was out there. By the time I went to East Tennessee State University, where I earned a master's degree in reading with a storytelling concentration, I knew that while I was different, I could learn. I was 59 years old when I began life anew as what else?—a storyteller and writer!

I now own up to who and what I am. I'm willing to share it anywhere with anybody if they want to know more. I am not stupid; I am different, and it's okay.

Discord

When passion's object departs,
bewildered nostalgia reigns.
Elusive at best,
love weighs heavy
on a hurting heart.

Seeking to fill a vacuum's agony,
one clings to remembrance
only to find dreams void of presence.

Some, and you were one,
love many times;
others, like me, succumb only once.

Our joining, frowned upon by all,
filled me with wonder and awe.
Then you were gone,
leaving me to ponder passions elusive—
stolen through death's ghostly touch.

Where once soothing chords strummed,
dissonance now reigns supreme,
our affection an obscure scent barely recalled.

The Glass Case

When the issue of integration first raised its head, it was difficult for most white folk in Tallahassee to understand why black folk made such a fuss—after all, everyone had their place in society, and place and appropriate behavior meant everything. Just as long as you minded who you were and where you were supposed to be, all was well in the universe. We still had separate water fountains and restrooms, and most hotels did not allow people with dark skin; restaurants were probably the most restrictive of all.

I recall the sit-ins at McCrory's 5 & 10. Both my parents worked downtown, so often I went to stay with them after school, stopping by for a root beer float at the 5 & 10. On that particular day, the lunch counter's clientele was decidedly different; well-dressed African-Americans had taken all the seats, and the servers were in a quandary about what to do. I watched from one of the aisles, afraid of what would happen to them, afraid for the servers if they got in trouble, afraid the effort might fail, and mortally afraid my dad would find out where I was. Eventually, they took the right to eat where they pleased, and received service, too, but I still can't figure out why they had to fight for it.

My father was a staunch segregationist and said things that still sear my soul to this day. He was kind to Annie, the woman who washed, starched, and ironed his shirts—before permanent press put her out of business—but to his way of thinking, she was decidedly not his equal. Annie, the only name I have for her, lived not far from the state capital in Smoky Hollow. Fog always gathered of an evening in the little dip near those homes, and Daddy always made sure we were there to leave his shirts and get out before dark. His fear transmitted to my brother and me, and it was always with relief that we left, but still, I didn't understand the reason for it. Now I know.

142

Charles was a young black man who worked at Putnam's Jewelry Store on East Jefferson. It was the same job my dad had when he was in his teens—vacuuming, sweeping, washing the windows, and keeping the glass cabinets sparkling at all times; only nobody offered to apprentice Charles the way they did my dad. He was a student at Florida A&M, and I always liked him. My dad was aware of our camaraderie, and this made Charles highly suspect in my dad's eyes.

Tallahassee's downtown stores used to close on Wednesday afternoons, but one day, an emergency repair sent Charles to our house. He approached the front door, and I opened it. Happy to see him, I hugged him just as I would any other friend of our family. The only problem was that my dad saw it—saw Charles, a black man, at our front door, holding his daughter! It's a wonder my dad didn't kill him that day; instead, he practiced what was probably even more difficult in a way—Dad humiliated Charles by sending him around to the back door and then dressing him down with words I couldn't understand at the time. It was awful, and Charles kept his distance after that. He graduated from college, became a professional man, and actually kept in touch with my father, but I lost his friendship that day and always resented it.

Change was slow in coming, but while my dad and grandfather continued to use the N word, eventually most of us learned to call colored people black, and later, African-American. When I was collecting oral histories for my book, *Southern Appalachian Storytellers: Interviews with Sixteen Keepers of the Oral Tradition,* I learned from storyteller Linda Goss why they had so many names. A respected Afri-lachian storyteller, Linda told me that in the past, the government, i.e., whites decided what to call them as a people, and that meant everything from the N word, to darkies, to coloreds. After Emancipation, the people began to rethink for themselves what they wanted others to call them and changed their minds often. They came up with some colorful names—black, African-American, Afri-lachian. More and white folks began the difficult task of respecting those choices.

Together, the people of Tallahassee lived through the assassinations of some of the greatest men America had produced up to that time—John F. Kennedy and his brother, Robert, and Martin Luther King, Jr., Malcolm X, and many others. We took the greatest care to cultivate the illusion that our town was immune no matter what happened in the outside world, but prejudice refused to die in spite of the new ideas that seethed around us.

Our schools were integrated but not without pain. I was a junior at the FSU Lab School, and my first experience up close and personal was my desk mate. His name was Marlon. Tall, well built, and self-assured, he never betrayed any lack of confidence around me, and we made friends quickly. Marlon confirmed what I had thought all along— scratch us, and we all bleed red; skin color is a superficial difference. It's what we think about it that gives us trouble.

When Barak Obama was elected President of the United States, I was living in Jonesborough, Tennessee, and decided to write a man-on-the street type of article. However, few African-Americans live in that area, so failing to find any African-Americans on the street, I made appointments to meet with them. One man in particular touched me deeply when I asked him about the label, "colored."

"I think about separate water fountains and restrooms when I hear that word. Don't use it, please." I never used that word again, but his response lingers unspoken in the back of my mind because I can still see the tears in his eyes.

Dandelion's Gold

Overnight
a grassy meadow played
to a musical score,
lines filled with yellow notes.

No longer a sedate green field,
it was filled with dancing polka dots
that brought a smile to my face
and warmth to my heart.

How could I not grin
when the good cheer of those
bright buttery orbs beckoned me
to come over and play?

Weeds somebody said, but to me
they were pieces of gold,
small nuggets of blessing.

Each petal a fleeting gift
born of Mother Earth and
blessed by Father Sun

.

Due Diligence

I grew up in a house filled with timepieces of every description; exquisite pocket and wristwatches, mantle, shelf, and wall clocks covered every available surface. Unless someone took the time to care for them and gently wind each one, they were still. Once wound, there was comfort in the sound—tick, tick, tick or tick tock, tick tock.

Certified as a master watchmaker by the Bulova Company in 1948, my dad was also a certified gemologist. In addition to myriad clocks and watches of every description, miniature vials of diamonds, opals, emeralds, rubies, and sapphires lay nestled in exquisite wooden boxes on his shelves. Fussy charm bracelets and priceless diamond rings got the same attention he focused on fragile timepieces, but there was a difference. Chronometers, once set in motion, keep time whether observed or not; jewelry is largely in stasis until someone views it.

Often, I sat near him as he worked, watching his strong hands manipulate tiny metal screws and pins, or bend minuscule prongs over a stone. He toiled for hours on end at that bench, an 18-karat gold magnifying eyepiece attached to his glasses like a third eye. Infinite patience and precise placement were essential to ensure that each timepiece kept accurate time. In some cases, lives depended on the diligence of one bald headed man sitting hunched over his bench.

Today tiny screens filled with more information than anyone could possibly need, light up 24/7, demanding immediate attention and response; only the lack of friends—or failure to pay the bill, are acceptable reasons for silence. So yes, things have changed in today's world. It's not all bad—thanks to cellular towers all over the world, we are accessible day or night, and it's no longer necessary to wind our new timepieces.

For all this supposed convenience, we are never alone and seldom allowed a moment to be still. No wonder we're run ragged most of the time! While it seems next to impossible to get off this track, doing so on occasion can make our transitory time on the planet a much more pleasant experience, but it takes work to make it happen.

I practice turning the phone and my laptop off and try to forget them for a while. You can read a hardcover book—feel the pages and smell the paper and travel to the mysterious places of the mind. Practice listening to the wind coming from far away or going you know not where. Taste the sweet tartness of wild blueberries, picked by the river or pick up shells by the ocean or seeds and rocks in the woods. Listen to the sounds of water rushing down steep slopes, cutting through solid rock to land in rivers deep and wide. Feel the soft green moss on your bare feet. Find a smooth, rounded river rock, and pay attention to its surface, its heft. Give it a toss, or take it home. Try settin' on a tree stump for a while, just thinking.

Lie in the grass late at night, watching stars and meteorites on their timeless journeys. Feel tiny ants crawling on your legs as dampness seeps through your clothing; sleep soundly, lulled by night sounds coming through an open window. Awaken to birdsong, the rising sun warm on your skin.

This prescription for life awareness requires periodic tune-ups to prevent atrophy, but it may take some serious time spent on the stump to get there. It takes due diligence to make it in this life, and sometimes we find it necessary to stop and reassess what we want out of it. We experience contrived time beyond our capacity to endure its artificial pace, only to wonder why we're so tired and depressed at the end of the day.

I've often wondered how my dad worked all day at the jewelry store downtown and then came home to work into the night on his clocks and watches. The only thing I can think of is that he found something that gave him great fulfillment, that to do it right, to hear the lovely sound of a watch keeping perfect time was music to his ears, but he was not a slave to it. When he went fishing, he completely left it behind. Gone were the starched dress shirt and tie, formality given way to comfortable khakis and the ridiculous blue fishing hat he loved to wear. When he returned, it was with new eyes that he beheld his timepieces. On the rivers and lakes, he tuned himself to nature, and when he returned, refreshed and ticking quite nicely, all was well.

Suspension

Morning's sun dawned on a world turned white.
Eerie shapes etched in snow,
bare trees traced bizarre shadows
against which bright birds flit.

Tufted titmouse, chickadees, Carolina wrens,
cardinals,
red as blood,
females glowing rusty pink and tan,
hairy woodpeckers
perched upside down,
feeding.

One lone leaf held tight,
suspended by merest thread
of woody stem,
easily broken.

Toni Boyd Wise Woman

A child of the South, I struggled with all of the prejudices with which I was raised. I thought myself successful in dealing with them, until my daughters were assigned to a school with a less than admirable reputation in a minority neighborhood.

With shame raging in my breast, I tried to move the family to a different school district, thus protecting my precious girls from harm and insuring the quality of education I felt necessary to successful lives—but it was not to be. They had to attend that school, and none other, and I agonized over it. It was not until an old friend paid a visit that I understood the task ahead and knew myself to be well equipped to deal with the situation at hand. I just needed an attitude adjustment from someone I trusted.

Toni Boyd was a former schoolteacher and the mother of three children when I first got to know her. Bill, her husband, was a professor at Florida State University. They were our next-door neighbors for many years, and I was their babysitter. The influence Toni had on me was profound from the beginning—she was erudite and yet so very human. I wanted to be like her when I grew up, but it was not until I met her again many years after my own marriage and the birth of my daughters that her influence really came into play.

When she learned I named my first child Kitty, after her daughter, she wanted to meet her. We were so surprised and happy to have her visit, and I knew it was ordained; she could help me find a way out of that school. Wisely, she listened as I poured my heart out. She saw my embarrassment and fear and said nothing until I was finished; then she said her piece. I will never forget her simple words because they altered my way of thinking in an instant.

"Saundra, do not fear for your daughters," she said, looking straight at me. Then she uttered the simple words that changed my

150

outlook on the situation: "They will get what they need because *you* will see to it that they do."

I saw it then; I had allowed what seemed like a no-win situation to toss me in the wind like broom sage, instead of taking stock and dealing with it. Because of her belief in my ability to make a difference, I became a strong presence at that school, volunteering in classes and for trips, and shoring up tired and underpaid teachers and the school's overworked administration. In addition, I got to know those students as children growing up under difficult circumstances, who were moving beyond it with pride in themselves and their school.

And, yes, I gave my girls every opportunity I could find, and it paid off, just as Toni said it would. My daughters won scholarships to universities, and both are now successful professional women, due in large part to Toni Boyd, a wise woman whose words changed lives.

Late Winter Snow

Sugar maples outside my window pulsate with new life,
tender buds pink like nipples on full warm breasts,
yearn for summer's heat.

Snow falls from a sullen, thick gray sky
earlier predicted to be blue.
Soft fat flakes coat every curving, sensual branch.

A black and white chickadee
staying in one place a second too long,
dons a fluffy white cap.

A family of cardinals,
their rich ruby red feathers
a vivid contrast to purest white,
mounts guard on feeders
ignoring downy woodpecker's eager approach.

Five soft-brown mourning doves feed below,
oblivious to the drama played out above,
gentle murmurings providing comfort
to all.

Secret Places

Some years ago, a hidden cove called me. Staying in a lonely cabin deep in the forest, I hoped to see a moose and nearly missed the gift I was meant to have. On a stroll to the shoreline, haunted by a magical Loon's cry, I stumbled into that place. Earth Mother greeted me with an enchanting medley, enveloping my soul in moss-encrusted arms. It was no accident—I knew the songs well, having sought out places like it in the past.

As a child, the notion of escape consumed me. Escape from a domineering grandmother, severe and tall, escape from a mother obsessed with beauty, and escape from church, the place of unobtainable perfection. My mind soon became the place of escape. Later, nature melded with it, granting peace.

Clandestine places tucked away in the woods called me as if by name—places where I could create imaginary worlds virtually untouched by reality. I recall the day I found nature's mysterious wealth hidden near my home. That shadowy place named me—I know this—how else did I find it? With pounding heart, I crossed the line—a busy, hot, asphalt freeway, and made my descent into glorious fantasy. An ancient sinkhole, seemingly wild and untouched, awaited my coming. It was as though I might be the first to find sacred space in its depths. At its center, an artesian well bubbled out of Earth Mother's belly—clean, pure, and free.

Sunlight gained dappled entry through nature's dense canopy to sparkle on dancing, clear, cold water. Verdant flora—avocado, lime, emerald, moss, and jade shimmered before my dazzled gaze, fragrant when crushed underfoot. I went there often, finding in that secret glade what my soul so desperately sought, a place of personal freedom and peace.

153

***

Now, many years later, the color green in all its vast panoply of shades continues to draw me into clandestine places of meditation. In that space, nurtured by Earth Mother's spirit, my soul flies unfettered, unrestrained—it is where whimsy and creativity reign supreme.

I have learned sometimes to look up into the canopy of trees to draw comfort from their enveloping embrace. What can be more wonderful than an azure sky seen through leafy limbs grown wide? An old live oak etched against night's sky, long, draping fronds on tall palms through which green ferns stream down. Trunks scaled in rich, gnarled tapestries of bark beg to be touched. Come. Come with me there.

Reflections Over Water

A rainbow shimmers
in the distance—
transient, translucent,
a color-filled scrim
hovering over dark,
gray waters.

Dolphins
play beyond—
dancing shadows
under nature's filmy bow,
wild bohemians worshiping
at the foot of an ephemeral crescent.

Life of a River

Rivers are the places of dreams. Their mysterious waters reflect the sun, moon, and stars, providing endless fascination. We drink the water and eat the fish rivers provide, and then we use them for power, manufacturing, transportation, hauling, and sewage. Aliens with arms and legs, we play in rivers, reap their bounty, and then deposit our sins in them through the ritual of baptism....

Water is a precious resource that we use and abuse with covetous abandon, staking claim to it as by right.

One of my favorite streams is the Apalachicola. Its source bubbles up from Earth's belly in North Georgia as the Flint River. From there, the long silver finger meets the Chattahoochee from Alabama, and then flows into Florida as the Apalachicola. It is a seamless, life-giving process, and one that without interference could continue far into the distant future, but man cannot allow that to be.

From its source in Georgia, all the way down to Florida where it empties into the Gulf of Mexico, the water's flow has been restricted. Held back in Georgia's huge Lake Lanier reservoir, it is a miracle there is any water left by the time it reaches Florida's state line. Once it arrives in the Land of Flowers, the river is dammed to create hydroelectric power. Huge piles of sand on the river's edge and blocked sloughs, bear testimony to the dread consequences of dredging.

Tenacious, the old river eventually finds its way to the Gulf, providing some of the world's best oysters in one of America's last pristine estuaries.

Nature's requirements are often set aside in favor of our immediate needs and desires. Some time ago, the Nature Conservancy listed the Apalachicola River as one of the "10 most endangered rivers in the country." In spite of its native and bountiful beauty, the 524-mile long river is at the epicenter of an endless controversy concerning the allocation of water between the states of Florida, Georgia, and Alabama. The fight is a bitter one with all three states claiming ownership of something to which they have no right. While state lines are arbitrary, the river owns its path—who are we to disturb it?

The Apalachicola, Chattahoochee, and Flint River system (ACF) has managed to adapt to most of the pressures we have placed upon it, but today, its fragile infrastructure is in need of support. Finding a balance of water allocation for human use and water for the ecosystem is crucial to the health of the river and the humans who use it. To protect it, however, we must learn both restraint and wisdom while providing reasonable access. Nature could be our teacher, as she has a way of finding balance, creating a perfect symmetry out of disorder. When left alone, order prevails, even in the wildest of places.

There remains unique beauty on the river in spite of man's well-intentioned interventions. Many years ago, I took my daughters out on the Apalachicola and down some of its creeks, like Scipio and Saul's, to give them a taste of the place.

Fish jumped, trees swayed in the wind, and living, dynamic water lapped against dense shorelines. Thick roots knitted together like old brown fingers held the water in its channel, roots that were still there after the great floods that once periodically cleansed and nurtured the land. Fabulous sabal palms, their fronds forming green bouquets at the top of sensuous curving trunks, grew in staggered ranks among young cypress, their brightness a rich contrast to the darkness of the forest. Beneath it all, palmettos, elegant ferns, and white spider lilies spread their wealth in reckless abandon.

I will never forget the marvels of that day on the old river—a day when I felt as though an essential part of me returned to itself just from being present. Green in every shade imaginable still plays before my eyes when I think of it; the gentle rhythm of the river moves my soul.

Rivers live and breathe, not as we do, but in accordance with nature's principles. Nothing is by accident. Our great North Florida River, the Apalachicola, is a symbol of continuation and completeness, of peaceful coexistence with the earth.

All is not well on our river, however. There is reckless destruction even today, a day when we know what loss of habitat causes—a day when we are more than just aware of what we are doing when we dredge or change the course of a waterway. Unfortunately, the person with the most dollars usually wins—not the cause of right, balance, or even need.

Dredged, gouged, stopped up, and then used as a dumping ground and a major highway, the Apalachicola River, deprived of its ancestral life's blood—water—is in danger. What is a river to someone who lives far from it, gets their water from a tap or in a bottle, and buys their oysters frozen in a bag, or served in a restaurant?

The minute we begin tampering with the environment, be it water, air, or soil, there are consequences. Let this be a reminder: it is we ourselves we must manage.

Lost Mountain

Some say
of what use is a mountaintop
when underneath lies
vast wealth—
hard, black, bituminous coal and gas,
energy for me and
profit for you.

Heedless of ultimate cost,
blow it up they say,
use what's there for the taking

But I say
once expended,
gone forever.

A legacy left behind of illness,
poverty, and ruin for some.
Children dead from rare cancers,
communities lost,
vistas gone,
energy spent.

Mountains where the soul once soared…
vanished.

Fair Weather, My Friend

On occasion, a snowy white egret used to visit my house on the Gulf coast of North Florida. A tall, slender bird, it was completely at home there, and although cautious, unafraid of me. Graceful and truly as white as newly fallen snow, he had been a frequent visitor for years prior to my arrival. The former owner told me the great, white bird had even been on the screened in porch.

I'm a great believer in wild things being wild, so I figured I'd let Snow get back to being a wild bird when I moved in, but it didn't take long for the big white egret to retrain me.

Try standing in your kitchen, back to the window, only to feel a presence staring a hole through your back; then turn around to find a big, white bird with a long, yellow beak perched on black, bamboo sticks staring at you from the deck. I can assure you, it would take very little time for you to enter servitude as I did. Soon, I rushed to provide food when he graced me with his presence, snatching food less than an inch from my finger, even though my determination remained not to be a regular provider—I really didn't want this wild bird to be dependent on me. I was, however, thrilled and honored to share his space every now and then.

Cruising in at a low altitude, he perched on the deck railing on occasion, a guest very sure of his welcome. He seemed drawn to cooking odors. Standing there, perched on one shiny, black bamboo leg, the other tucked up underneath his body, he waited patiently, a strong presence compelling my notice. Dropping everything to pay him homage, I rushed out with fish, shrimp, ham, or turkey, eager to please the royal bird. He wasn't fussy as long as I offered meat of some kind.

Snow's beauty stirred me up close and from afar. That I could be inches from such a wild creature, whose long, yellow beak had nearly

160

plucked food from my pale hand, amazed me to no end each time it happened.

That first spring I noticed Snow was changing. The yellowish membrane surrounding his beak turned a bright turquoise; his feathers seemed to lengthen and fluff to spectacular beauty. Snow was getting ready for mating season! I felt like a concerned mom. When he disappeared for several weeks, I worried about him and wondered if I would see the great, white bird again. It's odd how much I missed the egret who had befriended me.

The great blue heron continued to perch in the pines across the canal; his crazy-making caws made me laugh, but still, no Snow. When he finally returned after a couple of weeks—it was merely a flyover— he was in the company of another snowy white egret. His mate, perhaps? They declined to stay—just stopped by. I never saw any baby birds, just those two white, majestic beauties.

Eventually, Snow returned as a lone bird. For the longest time he stayed almost hidden in a sea pine across the canal. I can only assume he was molting because when he finally came to see me again, his fabulous mating plumage and bright, blue-green coloring were gone. While I had missed him, I rejoiced in his wild mating, glad to know he was free and that he had chosen to return.

When I moved away from Florida's coast, I looked back to see Snow atop the highest hip of the house, a weather vane telling me all was well in our world.

Fair weather my friend, fair weather.

Heat

Take it off, I said,
and wonderful things happened.
I don't know anymore, I said,
and the heat intensified.
I can't take it I said,
and the furnace grew hotter still.

I looked for someone to stand with me there,
an angel in my lion's den,
but my angel is yet to be
seen heard or felt.

Only the green of nature soothes my pain,
covering my soul with cooling salve
giving rest and sometimes
Peace.

An Affair of the Heart

My mom and dad were lovers. Best friends for most of their marriage, they provided an example I found impossible to replicate.

They met when Mom was sixteen and still in school. Dad was seven years older, already a man of the world, and I'm certain my mother found him glamorous in those early days; he was one of the few men she knew who was not a farmer, having abandoned the land not long after his father's death.

Sandy, worn-out farmland held little appeal for a young man with adventure on his mind and a family to help feed, so he headed to town. He soon found work sweeping the store and cleaning windows at Putnam's Jewelers in Tallahassee. Seeing in him a propensity for all things mechanical, Putnam's acculturated the young farm boy and apprenticed him as a watchmaker.

Mother—Dad always called her Millie—was a dreamer and an avid reader, who longed for the bigger world outside her tiny community of Waccissa, Florida. She was dating a handsome man named Milton when she met Ferd Gerrell, but it wasn't long before the skinny, freckled redhead got her attention. At five feet and two inches, she was a gorgeous young woman, a brunette with dancing, hazel eyes, and he simply couldn't resist her. That's when the letters began—he refused to be stymied by the twenty miles of poor, sandy rutted road that separated them. With other suitors competing to hold her hand in his absence, the United States Post Office was the most reliable means of holding them at bay.

Almost fifty years later, when death finally parted them, my brother and I were shocked to discover a studio portrait of Milton underneath piles of fabric when we cleaned out their home. While I am certain of my father's place in my mother's heart, it was obvious Milton held a special place there, too.

Mother was eighteen when WWII began, and like many other young women, she wanted to do her part in the war effort. She boarded a train and went down to Miami to Florida's only school of nursing, leaving Daddy bereft of his beloved and unable to join the fight himself. He wrote her almost every day (I have a stack of love letters— she probably saved them all) telling her of his travels to enlistment centers in Florida, Alabama, and Georgia. He had flat feet and a kidney ailment, and at each one, no matter how much he argued, he rated a 4F status. He poured out his disappointment in those letters and pleaded for her return; she turned a deaf ear but kept the letters.

The social life in glamorous Miami of the forties must have been exciting to the young country girl. From other letters I have read that were sent to her, she enjoyed the social scene, as well as collecting big conch shells from the beaches—many of which I still have in my possession.

School, however, was not without its problems. While she enjoyed her studies and loved the patients, the sight of blood gave her pause. When she reached surgical training and fainted dead away each time she saw red, she realized it was time to call it quits and go home.

Shortly after, bags packed and letters secured, she boarded the train and headed back to North Florida. According to my dad, he thought they would get married soon after her arrival, but he was mistaken—the lady had a mind of her own and things to do. She took a job with the Bell Telephone Company as an operator and enjoyed several years of relative independence before agreeing to marry him in 1944. They eloped on Christmas Eve, with Preacher Parker of the Pentecostal Holiness Church officiating, and drove to Marianna, staying at the Chipola, North Florida's grand hotel, for their honeymoon.

Mother always loved shades of turquoise, and her wedding dress was a bias-cut made of silk crepe in dusty aqua. I still have it, and the armature of her corsage. On their honeymoon, she wore a white, long-sleeved, embroidered, Mexican wedding blouse, but we'll speak of that later—both the dress and the corsage were stored with Dad's love letters and Milton's photograph in the cedar chest.

Was their marriage perfect? No, but their love was. One of the last things I remember that vividly bears testament to their enduring affection occurred just prior to her final passage.

Mom was in an extended care facility, having suffered a debilitating stroke, and hadn't spoken in a week. We were all there—Daddy, my brother Don, and I, when a tall, blonde woman entered the room. Dad obviously knew her, and it was just as obvious that he was shocked to see her there.

As it turned out, they had gone to the same elementary school, and although we had never heard of her... she knew both our parents. When she heard Mother was dying, she gussied up and came to pay her respects. She was a handsome woman in good health, and she flaunted it for my dad with Mother lying there comatose in the same room!

He gave her no encouragement, but there seemed to be no stopping the woman, so we did what polite Southerners know how to do best: we froze her out. She finally gave up and left, but when she did, we got a shock.

"Ferd," said my mother—the same woman who had not spoken in a week—"are you going to get married again when I die?"

For a moment, Daddy was speechless, but then he drew close to her and said, "Millie, I love you, and I always have. I will be married to you for the rest of my life."

Not long after, my brother and I were standing around her bed when Mother drew the last breath of precious life, pressed our hands, and departed. When we laid her to rest, she was dressed in a white, long-sleeved, embroidered Mexican wedding blouse at Dad's request.

My dad, always a man of his word, kept his promise. He was married to Millie for the rest of his life.

Fallen Stones

Wild violets grow where light feet once ran,
now we stumble on fallen stones covered
with messages of unknown origin.

Lavender, purple, and white,
tiny flowers dance on graves long forgotten,
feeding on ancient mitochondria.

Pick a violet, ask a question:
who lies beneath these stones—
black, red, or white;
man, woman, or child?

Violets arrayed in shades of mourning
know,
but will never tell

Snow on the Mountain

In 2009, I spent the Christmas holidays in Tallahassee, Florida, with my family. Leaving much later than I should have—it's so hard to leave loved ones—I made my way north, heading for Jonesborough, Tennessee, and my life as a storyteller and author. The drive was easy even though it was a holiday, so I made the decision to continue as night fell.

I recall pulling into a drive-through for coffee and receiving a call from my good friend Marjorie. Knowing me to be on the road and having just seen the weather report, she urged me to pull into a nearby motel and stay for the night.

No, I thought. *I'm too close—Jonesborough is just over the mountain. I will be all right.*

Just after I left Asheville, North Carolina, snowflakes lit up the night sky. On I drove, thinking I could stop in Mars Hill—there's a Comfort Inn there, but simple things are often complex, as was the case on this adventure.

I soon discovered myself driving in a severe snowstorm with almost zero visibility. When I got to Mars Hill and took the exit, it was to find banks of snow and ice. The Comfort Inn's drive was at least two feet deep in snow already. I knew my little Honda would never make it up that hill, so I crept back down to the interstate, slipping and sliding on the ice and driving snow on the mountain pass. Instead of turning back to Asheville and the probability of shelter, I turned left and continued toward home.

Once committed by my foolish decision, it was necessary to continue the trek over the pass slipping and sliding at 20 mph. There was literally no place to stop or turn around. It was go forward or pull over into a snow bank as others had done, turn my car into an igloo, and wait on the roadside.

Something in me said this particular Florida girl, who at that time knew practically nothing about snowstorms and icy conditions, could not afford to stop.

Soon all-wheel drive vehicles flew past, showering me with ice and snow, as I struggled to maintain a steady speed. I made every effort to stay on the tracks made by others, which soon became a major challenge. I learned fresh snow was easier to navigate than icy ruts, but it was difficult to see where the road actually was. I passed vehicles struggling to stay on the road, while others were already stuck in the snow banks, teetering on the edge of nowhere.

Salvation came in the form of fast-moving snowplows. I soon discovered pulling into their wake gave me better driving options, so each time one flew by, I slid into position behind it. That worked for a while, but since snow was literally pouring out of the sky, I quickly lost sight of them. I found myself blindly navigating through savage beauty, fearful and yet, in awe.

Through it all, Public Radio was my salvation. Justine Thoms and *New Dimensions* on NPR kept me wide-awake and thinking with the "Flavor of Joy," followed immediately after by "Hearts of Space." That conversation, and then the music, lit up the night, enabling me to achieve a steady state of mind.

I found safe refuge soon after descending the pass and Sam's Gap. It was an experience to remember: a minute life-filled pod—the car, my dog, Geoffrey, and me on a life-changing journey of only sixty-seven miles that took three hours to drive.

That night, firmly lodged in my mind's eye, will remain with me always, massive cliffs molded in white blankets of snow, giant icicles draping every surface, and great distances with no light beyond that of the snow's eerie glow reflected in my headlights.

Thank you for taking that trip with me and sharing the joy of each moment.

Sister, Let me Share your Trouble

Sister, can I share your trouble,
walk down the road with you—
ease the burden on your back,
so we can both stay on track?

Brother, can I share your trouble?
Come and talk to me
as we travel down this dusty road
over land and sea.

Brothers and Sisters, let
us share our troubles,
cry together,
heal our pain—
we have only peace to gain.

Broken

The end of 2011—and the beginning of 2012—will remain indelibly inscribed in my mind as the time I was put on hold, suspended in a fog for what seemed like forever. In that haze, I learned to accept help with grace, and I learned to share my burdens without feeling sorry for myself.

Scheduled to work the afternoon shift and then go straight to a holiday party, December 6, I was dressed up in a brand new, red, black, and gold sweater, black pants, and my favorite Mary Jane shoes. It was raining hard when I got to work, so I sprouted my umbrella and made a dash for the door. I got through the icy parking lot into the doorway, stepped onto the mat, then onto the linoleum, and that is where my life took a change.

I don't think it's possible to describe that sudden transition, but let me try. When my foot touched that newly waxed floor, it connected with a tiny puddle of water—was that spot of water already there, or did it come in on my shoe? I will probably never know, but what I can tell you is that my right foot engaged in a dance I will never forget—I left three tiny scuffmarks behind—when it twisted and down I went, on top of it. Blinding pain followed, and I could not move. Fortunately, my director was in the office, heard me cry out, and came to my aid. All this to say, one can never know the direction life may take in an instant.

It felt like hours before authorization came through for emergency care. Having a hook and grip wrist bandage on hand, I wrapped it around the ankle, and using the umbrella, I hobbled to my car. Pressing the gas pedal was a challenge since my right ankle was injured, but I drove myself, and then made my way into the facility for diagnosis and treatment.

Hours later, eying the snowy, dark night, staff asked, "Who is going to pick you up?"

We had not discussed transportation… and I was in shock and could only think of getting home. "I don't have anybody. I will drive myself."

"You can't do that with a cast on your foot!" they protested, but not vigorously.

"Yes I can. Just help me to the car." I rode out to my car in a fine wheelchair, and with the help of two strong women, settled myself in, new crutches at my side, and started the car. It took very little time to realize the difficulty—I couldn't feel my foot nor could I gauge how much to press the gas pedal.

Finding a good deal of traffic on the road and myself more than a little rattled, I decided to take the back way home—over the mountain and through the woods. It was misty and snowy, black ice lurked under my tires, and speeding cars appeared out of the dark to swerve in my direction. I soon learned the trick was steady pressure, but it was a hell of a drive home.

It's just a good thing I didn't realize the worst was yet to come. Salt and snow crunched underneath as I drove up the one-way lane to my apartment. When I got into the parking lot, I realized I'd never make it up the walk to the door. Without thinking, the cast-bound foot applied pressure, and the little black Honda ascended an icy slope never meant for cars, coming to rest beside my apartment.

Once there, to save my life, I could not figure out how to get out, mount the crutches, and get to my door through ice and snow. That is when it dawned on me, a bit late, that I had a cell phone in my pocket. My neighbor Jim came slipping and sliding down the walkway to the rescue. He fussed mightily at what I had done, all the while assisting me as if I was a baby into my home.

That week was my first orthopedic appointment after which Jim, who drove me in my car, attempted to drive up the slope as I had done earlier. We tore at the grass, snow, ice, and rock, but that car would not take itself up that incline for anything. Thus began three months of folks walking in front of or behind me every time I left for a doctor's appointment or physical therapy. Talk about helpless….

Three months of what felt like house arrest left me chafing. Mr. Jim took me to physical therapy a couple of times a week, and I was faithful to the exercises, but just moving from one end of the apartment to the other was a huge challenge. I grew irritable and testy, longing for freedom of movement and independence. It was then I began to understand my new role—I was the one in need of care, not the provider, and I didn't like it.

From my thirties through my early fifties, I was a caregiver, first to my grandmother, then to my grandfather, and then later to my mother, and finally, to my father with the help of my beloved cousin, Patsy. All of those family members were dearly loved, kindly people who while they never complained, must have felt exactly like me. I came to regret some of my actions from that period and learned to accept a measure of imperfection from myself.

It was from my dad that I learned what it meant to do acts of kindness and receive them in kind. He was always doing something for people, especially older women who had no one to help in their time of need. I recall one, a professor who lived in an authentic English cottage near our house. She salvaged and disassembled that old house many years earlier and brought it over from England on a ship, lich-gate and all. She had it rebuilt near an ancient live oak and lived there for many years with a massive English bulldog for company. When she needed help, she called my dad. Then there was the elderly lady whose gutters clogged with a growing tree. My dad, who was older than she was, climbed right up there—he was seventy-five at the time—dug the trees out, cleaned and repaired the gutters, and then fell to the ground on top of his ankle—the right one, by the way—the same as mine. Without letting her know his trauma, he drove himself home and then to the doctor, ending up with pins and screws holding the ankle together. Folks gathered from far and wide to help him, bringing food, running errands, and sharing conversation for weeks on end. He entertained them royally, enjoying all of the attention, but when they left, one could sense his frustration. He had things to do.

Enforced leisure is hard to deal with, but it can be done with a measure of grace if one tries hard enough. I will never again doubt the nature of human kindness or my debt to them. After all, one never knows what the day will hold—live in the moment, and live it as if it were the last one.

Break of Day

My nearest neighbor is a mockingbird.
Every morning she wakes up at 6:15, and so do I—
her music brings light and happiness to my sleepy brain.

Geese that over-wintered nearby
fly over at seven,
their brash honking adds a note of humor to my day.

Carpenter bees, their droning pleasant in its own way,
gnaw busily on my house, creating new passages
where none should ever be.

An opportunistic woodpecker searches their leavings
beating rat-a-tat, tat
amongst ccdar shavings.

Maple trees in full bloom offer
pulchritudinous blossoms,
sensuous in their rich, red, ripeness.

White trilliums bloom in creek bogs—primitive, sparse
Wild azaleas, tantalizing in soft pink cutwork lace
grace our lake—it's spring.

About the Author

  Born in Tallahassee, Florida, Saundra Kelley is a multigenerational Florida Cracker who moved to the mountains of Tennessee and never went home again. Her art combines writing with the ancient tradition of spoken word. She is a professional storyteller, traveling America's highways and back roads sharing her love of that which makes us really human—our stories.

  Kelley is the author of three books: *The Day the Mirror Cried*, *Danger in Blackwater Swamp*, and *Southern Appalachian Storytellers: Interviews with Sixteen Keepers of the Oral Tradition*. She is also a part of the environmental anthology, Between Two Rivers, edited by Susan

Cerulean, Janisse Ray and Laura Newton. She has recorded one CD, *Legends of the Wild: Tales of North Florida.*

Saundra Kelley lives in the Storytelling Capital of the world, Jonesborough, Tennessee, with her miniature poodle, Geoffrey. She travels the Southeast and beyond, sharing original stories, myths, and folklore imbued with a twist of green; reverence and appreciation of mother earth are a part of every story she tells or writes. In addition are her workshops, Let's Build a Better Guild, The Perfect Emcee, Use of Vocal Expression in Performance, Back to the Basics in Storytelling, So, You want to Write a Mystery, From Oral Performance to the Written Page/From the Written Page to Performance.

www.saundrakelleystoryteller.com
saundrakelley@blogspot.com

CPSIA information can be obtained
at www.ICGtesting.com
Printed in the USA
LVOW10s1126110517

534123LV00001B/4/P

9 781940 869230